STRINGS

MARIE LIPSCOMB

This book is dedicated to Jack Black, because he deserves to be cast as the romantic lead.

STRINGS

ONE

She's a horrible person. The absolute worst.

Sitting in a gorgeous converted barn at a round, lavishly decorated table, listening to heartwarming speeches and already halfway through her third glass of prosecco, Jordan should be happy. Cascading fairy lights glitter from the ceiling, and the warm air is scented with the gentle sweetness of dried wildflower bouquets. She's surrounded by friends and one of them—one of her very best friends in fact — just got married to an amazing woman.

But the way Finn smiles, the way the corners of his eyes crease as he watches his new bride, Beth, his broad chest expanding with pride and adoration, turns Jordan's heart hollow.

As she stands for the toast, she smooths her hand over the curve of her hip, pushing a crease out of her dark green velvet dress. She chose the color because it popped with her lavender hair and the cool tone of her pale skin, but now… well, it's a little too on the nose.

For the past ten years, she has been Vixen's Wail's cellist.

Throughout all of it, Finn has played his drums behind her. A decade of friendship, of touring the country, and never once has she felt anything like this toward him.

She helped him prepare for the big day, accompanied him to pick out his suit and helped him rehearse his vows. She never expected to feel jealous. Never once did she see what she sees today.

Yes, she had always known Finn was handsome.

Sure, his smile makes her smile.

Okay, she'd looked forward to each day they'd get to hang out together… but this. This is unexpected. And it's torture.

She exhales sharply, raising her glass to toast the couple. Regardless of her absurd and frankly unwelcome new feelings, she hopes they have a long and happy life together; she really does.

"It's so beautiful." Mia smiles beside her as the guests sit back down. The band's lead singer sets her glass on the table and reaches beneath to hold her husband's hand. "Beth's gown is gorgeous, isn't it? Let's get married again."

August's eyes soften as he turns to his wife. "Okay."

"Okay?"

"What my queen wants, my queen gets."

The couple chuckle together and though it's undeniably sweet, Jordan averts her eyes before they kiss. But of course, since it's a wedding, there are couples everywhere.

On the next table one of Finn's cousins sits whispering with his girlfriend, his fingers stroking the underside of her forearm. He's big and bearded like Finn, a former fire watchman who found his soulmate while she was lost in the forest. Finn had told the band the story one night after practice, his eyes lighting up with a newly cemented belief that no matter the odds, if people are meant for each other, the universe will bring them together.

If only she'd known that maybe the right person was right there, all this time.

"You okay?" Mia places her hand on Jordan's forearm and gives her a gentle squeeze. "You're a thousand miles away."

"Yeah." Her throat is rough. She tries to clear it without sounding too obvious. "Just… It's been a long day."

"Weddings always are." Mia stands. Though her wedding look is a little more toned down than her onstage appearance, she's still every part the majestic goth queen with her braided hair set in an elegant updo and dyed a vibrant midnight blue. The black, mermaid-tail gown hugs her figure perfectly, every movement accentuated by glittering black crystals set into the silk. She casts her deep brown eyes over Jordan's half-empty glass and the empty one beside that. "Don't forget we're playing tonight."

Jordan nods reassuringly, hoping Mia can't somehow tell that she absolutely did forget. Vixen's Wail are playing a three-song set after sundown. She reaches for a water jug and fills an empty glass. There's no way she's playing this set tipsy, not with emotions running so high.

"Water already, Jordo?"

The voice at her back straightens her spine and sends heat flooding across her skin. Finn stands behind her, embracing Mia.

Okay, she can do this. He's still just Finn, still her friend. She won't let misguided desire spoil that.

Despite her nerves and the turmoil raging through her heart, she turns and smiles. "You don't want me pulling the focus from you by falling off the stage during our set, now do you?"

Finn laughs, an easy, inviting sound which warms her heart. "At this point, we'll take all the free entertainment we can get."

"I warned you, weddings are expensive," Mia smiles.

When Mia steps back and takes her seat once more, Finn glances up at his new wife, as though if he looks away for too long, he'll find out she was a figment of his imagination.

"It's worth it," he says.

Jordan's eyes begin to burn and her vision blurs. "I'm so happy for you," she manages to say before her throat closes. She clears it again and offers Finn a smile.

She's absolutely not doing this.

"Thank you," Finn says gently. When he places his hand on her bare shoulder and offers her a friendly squeeze, the warmth of his rough hands on her skin makes her heart jolt. He inhales sharply. "Oh, Mia, before I forget, I placed the ad for the vocalist like we talked about."

"Thank you." Mia smiles and raises her glass. "But stop working, enjoy your day."

"Vocalist?" Cold fear trails down Jordan's back. Her breath catches in her throat as she turns to face Mia. "You're leaving?"

"Fuck no," Mia laughs. "No, we have a few duets written for the new album. We're just looking for a guest vocalist."

Jordan breathes a little easier. The last thing she wants is for the band to split. Getting to work with her best friends, following her dreams, it's more than she ever hoped possible, even if they are still mostly playing venues with leaky ceilings and peeling paint.

Finn stands to his full height. "I'll catch you later. I want to try and get round to thanking everyone before the set."

"Yeah, see you later, Finn." Trying not to watch him

leave, Jordan picks up a napkin and distracts herself by folding it into a floppy origami fortune teller.

She hopes it's a temporary crush, and not something she'll have to deal with every rehearsal, every performance, every night she lies alone.

Unwelcome thoughts haunt her. If only she'd realized sooner, before he met Beth. If only there was a way to reboot a heart, to factory reset her feelings. But there isn't.

Frustrated, she scrunches the napkin origami and raises her eyes. Mia is watching her.

"I need to go to the restroom," the vocalist says with a smile. "Will you come with me?"

Anything to distract her from these inconvenient, unfair feelings. They head to the bathroom together and it isn't until the door is closed behind them, and Mia has checked both stalls to make sure no one is there to hear, that Jordan realizes anything's wrong.

"Something's upsetting you," Mia states, folding her arms across her chest.

Jordan leans back against the sink countertop and mirrors Mia's gesture. "It's nothing."

"No, no it's definitely something, and if it's what I think it is, you need to put a stop to it now."

"I—"

"He's married," Mia sighs.

She could deny it, but she has never been a convincing liar. Evidently her covert lingering gazes weren't quite as secretive as she thought. "I know."

"How long have you felt this way?"

Jordan sighs. "About five hours. I think. Maybe I felt something for longer, but I didn't know what it was until—" She shakes her head, laughing bitterly. "Until I saw him standing at the end of the aisle and wished, just for a moment, that I was the woman he was waiting for. And now I can't stop thinking about it."

Mia exhales heavily, drumming her matte, blood red nails against the warm, deep brown skin of her arm, fixing Jordan in an unwavering stare. "Jord—"

"I just…God, I want someone to look at me the way he looked at Beth when she was walking down the aisle." Defeated, Jordan sighs and lowers her gaze to the floor. "I know, I'm a shitty person."

"You're not. You're a good person, but your heart is acting like a total jackass." Mia laughs a little and Jordan can't help but smile at the absurdity of it. The singer holds her gaze. "You can't have Finn, love."

"I know. And I'd never try to. It's not something I have any intention of acting on, but…I didn't expect it to hurt."

Mia's lean arms envelop Jordan, and her senses flood with the gentle honeyed scent of the vocalist's perfume as she stands there and lets herself be held. It's been a long time since anyone hugged her. Her touch-starved heart draws on the warmth of Mia's embrace.

The vocalist releases a heavy sigh. "I hate to bring this up, but you remember you swore never to get involved with another band member. Ever."

Of course she does. Danny was the love of her life for all of three months, almost a decade ago. He was the band's guitarist, tall and bearded with long silky black hair which he would toss around while he played. Their relationship had been short and scorching, but the intensity of their breakup had almost burned up the whole band. She'd sworn then and there she would never date another musician, especially not a Vixen.

Jordan nods and sighs. "I know."

"Finn is nothing like him, but this would be even messier. If you want my advice, you need to find a way to forget about these feelings." Mia steps back and checks her makeup in the mirror above the sink. As always, it's perfect. "As your friend, I'm telling you this is unhealthy and it's unfair to both of you."

"You're right. I know."

Mia smiles but her tone is firm. "And as a Vixen, I'm telling you to snap the fuck out of it. Find someone to flirt with, or just hang out with us and try not to dwell on it. If you keep thinking about Finn, at best you'll torture yourself, at worst you'll destroy your friendship with him and tear the band apart."

Jordan nods and pulls in a deep breath, before turning to look at herself in the mirror. She looks good, great, even. The green dress hugs her curves and her long, lavender hair makes her feel like a mermaid. Like a siren.

Rubbing a miniscule speck of mascara from beneath her lower eyelashes, she stands upright, pulls her shoulders back, and sets her mind. She's going to get over Finn, no matter what. Keeping Vixen's Wail together is far more important than a silly crush.

"You look perfect," Mia smiles. "Do whatever you've got to do to get over this."

Awkward doesn't cover it.

Étienne stands waiting, dressed in his best and surrounded by complete strangers.

The same unwelcome thought that's been milling

through his head all day pushes to the front of his mind. Getting stood up always sucks, but since his date ducked on her own cousin's wedding to avoid seeing him, he's pretty mortified.

As a wedding singer—or rather *former* wedding singer—he's used to the environment, but of course, in the past he was always invited to be there. He doesn't know the bride or groom at this one, and he doubts they even noticed him. He was supposed to be a plus one. Now, he's a lone loser trespassing on these strangers' special day.

He shifts his weight as he stands behind the groom, waiting for him to finish speaking to a table of guests. Every minute he stands there is an eternity.

God, he hopes the guy is the gentle sort of giant. He's almost a foot taller than Étienne and built like a slab of granite, but he has to say something. For goodness' sake, he was dragged into the group photos after the ceremony, placed on the front row since at five foot five he's considerably shorter than the groom's family of colossi.

Étienne's gaze trails across the party, overwhelmed by the mass of strangers. There isn't a single familiar face in the crowd. Not one.

Some of the guests glance over at him, and a few of them look again. He basks in the boost to his temporarily wounded self-esteem. Years of performing on stage have taught him how to hold himself, how to project confidence and sex appeal. It helps that he's fully aware of how handsome he is; the way his dark lashes frame his blue-grey eyes, the way he's completely comfortable with his height and his sturdy, heavyset body. Étienne is used to being watched and wanted.

But his breath catches as one particular woman works her

way across the room, sidling past the tables and chattering guests. Her full, curvaceous figure is wrapped in green velvet, and her lavender hair tumbles down her back in shimmering waves.

She looks up, and his stomach flutters.

For a moment he thinks her eyes are on him, but no. It's the groom she's looking at as she takes her seat and sips a glass of water. Her gaze slides to the side, to the woman beside her giving her a don't-you-fucking-dare glare.

Interesting. Étienne's attention is dragged away as the groom turns and looks down at him.

The big guy's welcoming smile falters as his eyes narrow at the intruder. "Hi. Sorry, I don't think I know you."

Clearing his throat, Étienne's blood runs cold. "Ah, no. Um, I was supposed to be Krista's date—"

"Beth's cousin?"

"Right. Only she hasn't shown up, so I'm just, you know…"

The groom's eyebrows raise a little as he inflates his massive chest with a long breath.

Étienne braces himself. "I didn't think it was a good idea to tell Beth, you know, just in case she's upset over Krista." He pauses a second, waiting for the groom's reaction. The man's eyes flicker over to his new wife, before he gives a gentle nod. Okay, good, that was the right decision. Étienne clears his throat. "Anyway, I just came over to apologize for intruding and wish you a happy marriage."

The groom laughs a little, running his hands over the thick hair of his beard. "That sucks man, I'm sorry."

"Yeah," Étienne sighs, giving a little breathless laugh of his own. "To be honest, I feel like a complete loser."

He feels worse than that, honestly. The week started out

with the catastrophic implosion of his band, his life's meaning for almost six years. Things had been a little rocky over the past few months, but he'd hoped they could work it out. They were good, really good, but personalities weren't compatible, especially not with his guitarist.

Getting the date with Krista was the light at the end of a very bleak tunnel, but now he's dateless *and* bandless. "I'm going to head on home, but I hope you all have a great evening."

"You can stay if you want?" The groom shrugs and chuckles. "Your food and drinks are already paid for and I'm sure Beth isn't going to mind. Hell, you can eat Krista's too."

It's Étienne's turn to laugh as he scans the room. The other guests are chatting, smiling, and sipping free wine. He has nothing else planned. "It wouldn't be weird?"

The groom scoffs lightheartedly. "Not at all, the more the merrier. Fill your boots."

It's easy to like this guy. Right away Étienne can tell he's one of those people with the ability to make anyone feel instantly welcome, like they've been friends for years.

"Alright, thank you."

The groom shakes his hand and the rough calluses on his palms grate against Étienne's. He remembers vaguely, Krista telling him her cousin was marrying a drummer. Working with a guy that laid back would be easy. He highly doubts the groom is going to want to talk shop on his wedding day, but putting out some feelers for musicians can't hurt.

"I'm Étienne, by the way."

"Finn. It's good to meet you."

"Can I get you a drink?" Étienne chuckles. "A drink you've already paid for."

Finn smiles and looks around the room, assessing the

guests he hasn't yet spoken to. He looks happy, but exhausted. His broad shoulders relax. "Yeah, man. A drink sounds great."

Étienne leads the way, his mind whirring. Good drummers can be hard to find and if he's to put together a new band, finding his way into Finn's good books isn't a bad idea.

"Krista mentioned you're a drummer."

"I'm surprised she knows that much," Finn sighs, relieved as he slides onto a tall wooden stool at the bar. "But yeah." He glances at the bartender. "Scotch on the rocks please."

"Same, please," Étienne nods. He's not even a whisky drinker, hates the stuff, but he'll make an exception if it endears Finn to him. "Who do you play with?" He tries to sound casual, but his heart picks up its pace as anticipation settles on his chest.

The ideal answer is 'no one'. He'll take a 'yeah but they suck.' The worst possible answer would be—

"Vixen's Wail."

It's hard not to look crushed as the bartender pours their drinks. He's heard that name a few times, seen their posters around town. They're solid. Damn good vocalist too by all accounts. Their logo may as well be a huge no poaching sign.

"What do you do?" Finn asks.

"For a living?"

"Yeah."

Étienne takes a sip of the bitter, burning liquid. "Right now, not a whole lot. I'm a vocalist, but…you know, hard to be a frontman with no band."

"Oh, I'm sorry, that sucks."

"This whole week sucks." Étienne takes another drink and tries not to cough as he swallows. The taste makes his eyes water. "I'm sorry. I shouldn't be complaining to you on your wedding day."

Finn drinks too, tightening his lips over his teeth as he swallows. He frowns a little, milling something over in his mind before he speaks again. "Are you looking for someone to play with?"

A spark of hope begins to smolder in Étienne's chest. "You know someone?"

"We're actually looking for a vocalist to work with us on a few duets. Nothing full-time, but if you want to audition—"

"I do." Étienne knows he should play it cool, but a chance to work with Vixen's Wail could be the start of an exciting chapter of his career. His old band never played their own music. As much as he enjoyed those crowd pleasers, singing original songs is his dream.

Finn chuckles. "Hey, that's the second time someone's said that to me today."

It's impossible not to smile. This big, beautiful bastard is throwing him a lifeline, despite the fact he's a total stranger who effectively crashed his wedding. He could hug him. "Are you sure? I mean, the type of music I usually sing isn't exactly… What is it that Vixen's Wail does?"

"Symphonic metal."

"Right…" Étienne nods, but he hasn't a clue what any of that means. "I'm generally more of an 80s bops kind of guy."

"Are you good though?"

The question takes him aback. "Well, yeah but—"

"We're playing a set in about half an hour," Finn says. He pulls his phone out of his pocket and opens the contacts before handing it to Étienne to add his details. "Take a listen, see if you think it's something you can do and I'll text you the time and date and what's expected. The details are also on our website, you know, in case I forget." He raises his glass and grins. "To fated meetings."

Étienne doesn't want to let this guy see his hands tremble, but he can't help it. He's all but vibrating out of his damn skin with excitement as he puts in his number. The biggest gig his band ever played was as a support act for a marginally popular local band, but Vixen's Wail are on the cusp of a breakthrough. Their fans are loyal, selling out venues. This is big. Raising his glass to clink it against Finn's, Étienne can't help but smile. "To whatever comes next."

They drink together, and Étienne's body shivers at the bitter taste. When he finally gets about half the drink down, he slams it back on the bar.

Finn grins and shakes his head. "You don't have to drink it, dude. Let me get you something you actually like."

Relieved, Étienne sighs and picks up the short and sweet cocktail menu from the bar.

Two

It's no use. No matter how hard Jordan tries, her eyes constantly drift back to Finn. He seems perfectly at home surrounded by people, laughing, confident, shaking their hands, throwing his arms around them. He works the room, double-fisting whisky glasses, his cheeks rosy above his beard as he beams, making every guest feel welcome and wanted.

Finding someone else to distract her is a fool's errand. Right now, no one can come close to being as attractive as Finn. No one.

She almost has herself convinced as she forces herself to look away, toward the bar, and finds herself transfixed by the sight of a stranger.

From that angle she can just make out that the man's full, luscious lips are pulled into a genuine grin as the bartender hands him a bright blue cocktail in a tall glass. It's a bewitching smile, one she can't look away from. As he turns around, spinning the barstool so he can face the rest of the room, she sees him fully and he mesmerizes her completely.

He sits on the edge of the seat so his toes reach the chrome foot rest of the stool as he surveys the guests at their tables with a cool and calm gaze. He isn't very tall, but he's thickset, and solid, with slicked back, dark brown hair, and short, slightly rusty facial hair. The twinkling fairy lights hanging like a shower of stars from the ceiling cast a dappled golden glow over his pale, peachy complexion.

And oh boy, is he ever pretty.

On any other day she'd try to make eye contact and act coy until he approached her, but not today. The pain in her heart can only be soothed by one thing, and that is a toe-curling orgasm from this ridiculously handsome stranger. Jordan doesn't have time for coy.

Every cell in her body wants him. He would be an indulgence, she tells herself as she stands, a treat to help her heart mend. Nothing more.

She smooths down the emerald green velvet wrapped around her figure and makes her way over to the bar. The air of confidence she gives off is fairly convincing, she's sure, but inside her heart is flipping, tumbling. Is she really doing this? Thankfully the water has sobered her up a little, and the room is barely swaying.

The stranger glances at her as she draws close. Heavy-lidded eyes rake across her, cloud-grey and full of promise. It's a look which says, *"This is beneath me and if you ask nicely, you'll be beneath me too."*

Goosebumps tingle along her arms and each breath becomes a little harder to draw. Somehow, she keeps her gaze neutral as she slides onto a bar stool at his side. Fixing her eyes dead ahead, the onset of panic claws at her.

"Gin and tonic, please. Double. And a bowl of olives," she says to the bartender. It's ill-advised when she's already three glasses of prosecco down, but none of this is a particularly good idea. If she's going to fuck up, may as well do it spectacularly.

Whether it's wishful thinking or it's actually happening, she doesn't know, but the heat of his eyes trailing her figure turns her mouth dry. He doesn't say anything. Neither does she. The knot in her throat won't allow her to. What does one even say in this situation? She's so far out of her depth the waters are growing dark around her.

Abort mission. ABORT MISSION.

"Hi," he says. It's as simple as that.

She almost laughs, pressing her top teeth into her lower lip. "Hey."

S he's stunning, in every sense of the word. Étienne simultaneously thanks and curses every force in the universe for seating her next to him. Vibrant red lips, shocking against her pale white skin, part as she tugs her bottom lip with her teeth.

Why, *why* had he let Finn talk him into switching out the whisky for something he actually likes the taste of. He could've looked smooth and sophisticated, but no, that would require the universe to take mercy on him.

"So… How's it going?" he asks. He tries to sound casual, but he's fairly certain he's convincing no-one. It's rare for someone to make him feel nervous. He's a frontman after all, all swagger and hip-thrusts in front of an audience, but before a goddess, he's frozen and fumbling.

"It's… going." She sips her drink through a narrow stainless-steel straw and closes her hazel eyes. Her posture melts a little and stiffens just as fast, and she blinks as though only just realizing she's in the room.

Okay, so she's a little tipsy. That puts her way off limits and therefore much easier to talk to. "Groom's side or bride's side?"

She casts him a sidelong glance and gives a small, but undeniably bitter chuckle. "Groom's. You?"

He pulls in a heavy breath and leans onto the bar, sipping his blue lagoon through a vibrant pink curly straw. She watches him, a perfectly preened eyebrow raising before her red lips part again and her face brightens with gentle laughter.

"I guess technically the bride's side," he answers, secretly pleased with himself for making her laugh. "I was *supposed* to be her cousin's date, but her cousin didn't show up. I haven't actually spoken to the bride though, and the groom bought me the drink, so—"

"Ah so you're a defector?"

"Yes." He grins. "Team Finn all the way."

The smile falls from her lips. It doesn't take a genius to figure out there's some resentment there, some half-unraveled tangle of feelings. She slides the small, white bowl of olives between them and skewers a purple one on the end of a cocktail stick. "Help yourself."

He copies her, skewering an olive and popping it into his mouth. They're almost overpoweringly garlicky, which in this instance is definitely a good thing. Kissing this mysterious woman is the only thing he can think of, but not when they both have garlic breath and definitely not while she's drunk. Ridiculous, he tells himself, he doesn't even know her.

"What's your name?" he asks.

Her throat twitches as she swallows her olive and stares at

the wall of mirrors above the vast array of half-full bottles behind the bar. He can't blame her. All he wants to do is stare at her too.

"Do you know why she stood you up?" Her blunt question sets him back somewhat, not least because she refused to answer his. "Did she tell you?"

"No. I don't know. She just didn't show."

She smiles at him, a mix of tipsiness and sympathy he's simultaneously endeared to and frustrated by. Of course, he could speculate. Often, it's his height, the fact that some women seem to take issue with being taller than him when they're in heels. Occasionally, it's his weight. Neither of those things bother him and he'll be damned before he lets someone else's insecurities fuel his. He knows he's attractive. He doesn't need someone else to tell him so.

"Her loss," she smiles.

"Couldn't agree more."

They raise their glasses and clink them together before both taking a sip. Étienne catches sight of them in the reflection. They make a striking couple, both full-figured, both devastatingly beautiful.

"Are you here alone too?" His heart lunges as the question leaves his lips. He doesn't *do* flirting.

The woman looks down at her glass, spearing a wedge of lime with the end of her straw. Her smoke-lined eyes are intent on the task, as though the entire world consists of her and the lime.

"No," she says at last. "I'm here with you."

THREE

"My name is Étienne."

Jordan can't take her eyes off his full, soft-looking lips as he says his name. They're kind of pouty, and infinitely suckable. She could happily let those lips distract her for hours. They quirk up in gentle amusement as she stares.

"Étienne." The name dances on the tip of her tongue as she repeats it. "It's a nice name. Are you French?"

"No, it's a family tradition. But my grandmother came here from France."

"Really?"

"Yeah. She came here looking for love and found my granddaddy literally standing on the docks when she got off the boat. He asked for her papers and Mémé said she'd swap him for a drink."

"That's sweet." The gin is going straight to her head, making it heavy. She rests her temple on her fist and braces her elbow on the bar. "And it worked."

"Sure did. I come from a long line of hopeless romantics."

She likes him, likes his confidence. He's a little shorter than average, but solidly built. Not like Finn. Finn is an enormous, vaguely human-looking teddy bear. But this guy...if a gorilla and a peacock somehow mated and raised their unholy offspring on a diet of pure Kobe beef and condor eggs, it'd be half as solid as him and have only a fraction of the swagger.

Thick thighs too. Bitable.

"So, do you speak French?"

"Sure." Those lips lift again. He leans toward her, arching an eyebrow as he holds her gaze. Heat prickles across her cheeks as he comes closer, the faint spice of his cologne making her heart race harder. He's so close she would only have to lean in a little to kiss him. Briefly, his eyes flicker down to her mouth, and when they raise again, they're alight with roguery. "Baguette."

She stifles a laugh, biting into her lower lip. "That's hot."

He gives a humble shrug before a brief chuckle cracks his suave façade. Sitting back upright, he skewers an olive on the end of a cocktail stick. "Thanks."

Stealing a glance at him, her heart flutters. He's cute. Beyond cute. He has a face she'd happily spend half her life kissing and the other half sitting on, and a sturdy, husky body she wants to cuddle up to. They seem pretty compatible. Almost too compatible to throw away one a one-night stand.

Almost compatible enough for her to give him her name.

Guests gathering around the edge of the dancefloor draw Jordan's attention. They surround the happy couple, watching them take their first dance together. The way Finn looks at Beth, the absolute love and devotion in his eyes, retightens the knot which was loosening in her chest. She doesn't want this random guy, not really. She wants *that*.

But she can't have that. Not with Finn. Not ever.

She needs to fuck him out of her system.

She clears her throat and downs her drink, only registering that Étienne is looking at her when she sets the glass down on the bar top. "So, listen, I have a hotel room."

Étienne sighs deeply, as he runs his finger around the rim of his glass. A shiver courses through her body as she imagines that feathery touch on the inside of her thigh.

She drags her eyes away from his hands, back to his face, even as she begins to burn up. "Come back with me tonight, if you want to…"

"I don't even know your name," he says.

"I know. That's the point."

"Why?"

Her throat dries out. It's so out of character for her, so beyond her comfort zone, but then again, so is lusting after a groom at his own wedding. "Because I don't want you to be able to find me after tonight."

Étienne's eyebrows knit together as he places his cocktail stick on a napkin. "Wow." He laughs bitterly and the sound of it clenches Jordan's heart. "And here I was thinking we were getting along well."

"We are. I wouldn't ask otherwise."

"This isn't the compliment you think it is."

She doesn't want to offend him, she really doesn't. He's handsome, sexy, he makes her laugh, but she just needs a release, just for tonight. She's too raw, too confused. Anything more than just sex is too much.

Étienne stands and steps around the back of his chair,

putting it between them. "Listen, I don't really know anything about who you are, but I can tell you've had a few drinks—"

So that's it; he thinks she's drunk. She isn't. A little tipsy maybe, her inhibitions lowered, but she isn't so far gone that she doesn't know exactly what she's doing. He doesn't need to build a protective barrier between them. She's lonely and horny, not a savage beast about to tear into him. "No, that's—"

"And I know for damn sure, that hooking up with a woman at a wedding when she can't take her eyes of the groom is a bad, *bad* idea." His chest deflates a little as his lips part, conflict raging behind his blue eyes. "For both of us."

She bristles at his words. "What? What do you mean? I'm not staring at Finn."

"It's hard to miss…"

The burning heat of his accusation crawls beneath her skin, searing down to the core of her. "You know what? Go fuck yourself."

He sees through her hastily built defense immediately, his handsome face twisting into an incredulous smile. "Alright. Well, it was nice meeting you, have a good evening."

And with that, he turns and walks away.

"Wait—" She's a second behind him, her apology on the tip of her tongue when Mia grabs her arm.

"We need you," the vocalist says urgently. "It's time for our set."

The room spins and whirls around her as Mia tugs her away from the bar. As the women make their way toward the stage, Jordan watches over her shoulder as Étienne's stocky figure carves a path through the guests. He doesn't turn back, doesn't even seem to give her a second thought. And why should he? She was an asshole.

Deep down, she knows he was right. This is for the best. For both of them.

———

Every fiber of Étienne's body protests as he walks away from her, but he won't be anyone's consolation prize. He doesn't deny he's tempted. She's beautiful, and he'd love nothing more than to have her use his body for pleasure. But not his heart. No matter how gorgeous she is, or how tempting her offer, it isn't worth having his heart torn out twice in one day.

He can't go through that. Not after the week he's had.

Yes, okay he'll miss the Vixen's Wail set, but he has an idea of the kind of music they play. Not that it matters. At this point he'll join a damn yodeling group if it means he can get back out on stage and sing.

He pulls out his phone to make sure Finn sent the text with the details of the audition.

Wednesday, 11 a.m. The Mayfly.

He knows the place. It's a bar about a half hour drive from home.

A flutter of nerves turns his stomach. Three days. So little time to prepare for an audition which could potentially change his life. He's so excited and so nervous during the cab ride home, he momentarily forgets about the woman with the lavender hair. Almost.

When he gets home to his apartment, he takes off his suit

jacket and pants, hanging them carefully. He can't really afford to waste money on dry cleaning right now. He changes into a soft white t-shirt and grey joggers.

He knows just how lucky he is to even be able to pay his rent with the money he made with his old band but he's also all too aware those funds won't last forever. The thought of how much money he wasted on the cab ride home makes his heart canter. Sooner or later, he may have to admit defeat and find a job elsewhere. Unless he nails this audition.

With a sigh he settles onto the floor of his living room and pulls his clunky laptop out of its case, presses the power button and waits for it to load. He does his best thinking on the floor.

It's far too late at night to begin practicing for his audition, but he can at least listen to a few of Vixen's Wail's tracks and figure out the sort of songs he could sing for them. Imagining himself at the audition makes his belly flop. He can't shake the feeling that this is *it*.

He glares at the struggling, whirring, machine in his lap, growing ever more frustrated. One day he might have enough disposable income to buy something not on its last legs.

Vixen's Wail could be a step toward that.

He tries to hold on to that dream, the relief of not having to worry about money for a while, the thought of performing in front of a crowd. It should be all he can think about, but—

What if he'd taken the woman with lavender hair up on her offer?

The question rolls around his mind, evading every attempt to exorcise her. How would she have tasted? After she'd stripped away the velvet, would she be just as soft underneath?

Could he have dealt with being stood up by one woman, and used and discarded by another, all in one night?

He knows the answer all too well. He can't do 'no-strings.'

Still, he's thinking about her far too much. Imagining too much.

His jaw clenches as he types in his password and finds himself faced with his reflection in the black desktop background. At least he can stand to look himself in the eye.

Casting her from his mind, he pulls in a deep breath. He needs to focus on Vixen's Wail. The road to that destiny begins now. He's raring to go when a message asking him to restart his computer to install updates flashes across the screen.

"Fuck it."

He snaps it shut, and heads to bed.

FOUR

Jordan rolls away from the aggressive sunlight streaming through the hotel's flimsy blinds window, and wraps herself up in the duvet. The headache and shame hit her at the same time. Her tongue is wooly, her body aching. She'd spent the night singing, dancing, and ultimately cackling with Mia while sitting on a low stone wall at the back of the barn's parking lot while August called them a cab to take them to the hotel.

None of that is cause for embarrassment, but the guy at the bar is another story altogether.

Étienne.

God, she'd been so rude to him. The emotion, the alcohol, all of it… she lost control, and she hates that more than anything.

She half wants to track him down and apologize. He didn't deserve to be treated like that, as though he were disposable. But the other half of her knows she would quite simply perish if she ever laid eyes on him again.

There's a faint, persistent hum somewhere in the vast,

unforgiving world beyond her duvet fortress. Squinting in the light, she sees her phone vibrating on the nightstand. Whoever it is they can wait. It's Sunday and she has no intention of moving until she absolutely has to check out.

Eventually, the buzzing stops, and she's left alone in silence.

Left alone to wonder. What would it have been like, to wake up beside Étienne? Thoughts of that strong, sturdy body pressed against hers cloud her mind. Those lips. God, what she wouldn't give to be granted a second chance to feel those lips on her skin.

She closes her eyes as her phone begins buzzing again.

With a frustrated huff, she reaches out of her cocoon and grabs the petulant device. Mia's name flashes in the center of the screen, bright and painful and just too much.

"I'll call you back," Jordan grumbles as she sends the call to voicemail. As she lets it fall from her hand, she buries her head in the crook of her elbow.

She's almost back asleep, when a sharp knock at the door rouses her. "What?"

"It's Mia. Get up. I need to talk to you," the muffled response comes through the door.

Jordan groans as she rolls over. "I'm dead."

"So? Hurry the fuck up."

Pain shoots up Jordan's calves the moment her feet hit the ground. Dancing all night in her heels was a bad decision. Hell, last night was chock-full of bad decisions. Limping toward the door, she makes sure she's halfway decent before turning the lock.

As Jordan opens the door, Mia hands her a Styrofoam cup of coffee and winces at her appearance. "Damn. You okay?"

Jordan peers, eyes half-closed into the obnoxiously bright hallway and shakes her head. "No."

No matter how many hangovers, how many times she swears it'll never happen again, she always forgets not to mix grapes and grain. Her drunken logic of "gin has berries in it, so it's basically fruit," never saves her.

"We have to have a meeting. An emergency Vixen's meeting," Mia says.

Jordan's eyes widen. Did she do something bad last night? Did she say something irredeemable? "Is everything okay?"

"Everything's great." Mia's smile lets her tension ebb. "Can you be downstairs in twenty minutes?"

In a body bag, maybe?

Jordan nods as she sips the coffee. It's filled with hazelnut flavored creamer and packed with sugar, just how she likes it. "I'll be there in fifteen."

Mia claps her hands together and flashes a nervous, but excited smile. Something's going on. Something Jordan is far too delicate to try to fathom right now.

She heads back to her room, and all but crawls into the shower. She closes her eyes as she lets the water beat against her, and all she can picture is Étienne and the way those soft lips parted as she asked him back to her room, and the way he put his chair between them, as though she was some ravenous beast about to pounce.

A fresh wave of shame hits her as she squeezes her eyes tight shut. At least she never has to see him again.

Twenty-five minutes later she heads downstairs.

"You're serious?" Étienne is trembling, one hand clutching his phone to his ear, the other gripping a fistful of his hair. "Today?"

"If it's at all possible. As soon as you can." Finn sounds exhausted on the other end of the phone. Poor guy. It's his first full day as a married man and he's working, trying to put together a last-minute audition. "I don't want to say too much until it's all finalized, but an opportunity has come up and we need to get this ball rolling as quickly as possible."

Étienne paces back and forth across his living room, his heart lunging against his ribs. He hasn't prepared. Shit, he doesn't know a single one of Vixen's Wail's songs. He's never even heard them. Three days was cutting it fine, but this… this is nuts.

But as his dad always taught him, if you can't blind them with brilliance, baffle them with bullshit. "Yeah man, no problem. I'll be there in about an hour."

"Sweet. We're at a hotel, not the Mayfly. The Hillcrest hotel."

"I know it."

"Awesome, thanks so much, Baby Bear. See you later."

"Yeah, later." As the call ends Étienne can't help but grin. They're already at the nicknames stage. It's a good sign.

He hurries to the bathroom to shower and clean himself up, all the while running through vocal warm-ups.

Fifteen minutes later he's heading to his little blue hatchback, downloading Vixen's Wail's album onto his phone so he can listen on the journey. He turns the key in the ignition and is met by a shrill, grating wheeze, and complete stillness from the vehicle.

"Do not," he sighs as he sharply taps the steering wheel. "Don't you dare. Not today."

Taking a deep breath, he turns the key again. His heart sinks as the whir returns.

"Fuck," he seethes, sitting back against the seat. He rasps his fingers through the short coarse hair on his cheek. "Please, *please* just don't be shit, for once, for me. Please. If I get this gig, I can pay for repairs, I can get you fucking velvet seat covers and clean the bird shit off of you. Just please… work."

The next turn of the key is rewarded with a joyful growl, as the car comes to life. Giddy with relief, Étienne gives the engine time to turn over before clicking the AUX cord into the headphone jack of his phone and pressing play.

He sits for a moment as the music kicks in, a chill rolling through his body. The deep, somber sound of a cello, winds through the air, beautiful and heartbreaking. He rubs the back of his neck, soothing the hairs standing to attention and tries to ignore the flutter of nerves in his belly.

It's hard to imagine a man as laid back and ursine as Finn playing in this theatrical, vampiric band, but when the drums kick in, he can't help but grin. That's definitely the big guy. Every element of their sound is tight, precisely fitted cogs in an exquisite machine.

He sets off and tries to see himself fitting in there, wedging himself into all that precision. All the while the hairs on his arms stand on end, like snakes charmed by the low, melodic lament of the cello.

But when the vocals start, he damn near dies of terror.

He knew their singer was good, but shit, she's phenomenal, otherworldly, classically trained and a thousand leagues better than he could ever be. By the time he pulls up at the

Hillcrest hotel, his heart is in his throat. He's going to look like a complete jackass.

He can't sing in that state, not so tense and fraught.

Listening to their album, he's not actually even sure he can sing at all. It seems he's just been shrieking and grunting for the past twenty-five years.

"Alright, get it together." He breathes deeply and puts his head back against the headrest.

Closing his eyes, he focuses on the darkness behind his eyelids, and works on keeping his breath steady. The music blares at him, theatrical and beautiful and intimidating as hell. He's never had stage fright, never, not even in the early days when he was ten-years-old singing on his school's stage during battle of the bands. He has never felt this terror.

But then, he's never been in a situation where so much hinged on his performance in an audition.

He's about to turn the key in the ignition and call the whole thing off, when the music begins to decrescendo. The drums and vocals stop, the guitar and bass drop out, the keyboard, the violin, until all that's left is the cello. It resonates deep, soothing his tension like a loving caress. He loves that sound, loves how it rolls through his body, pebbling his skin. It cradles his soul.

He can breathe again. Shaking loose his shoulders he knows he can do this.

He can audition for Vixen's Wail.

It isn't just the hangover making the information hard to process. Nothing Mia says is making sense. Jordan rubs her forehead with her fingertips. "Is this actually happening?"

Mia claps her hands together and beams. "Yes! Finn got the call this morning. Phantom's Run were meant to headline Ghoulfest but they had to drop out, so we're taking their place."

The rest of the band look at Jordan expectantly. She was the last to arrive at the meeting, as usual, and the last to hear this life-changing news.

"We're headlining a festival?"

Finn laughs, smoothing his hands over his head. "I know. It's…god…it's a dream come true."

"But how… we weren't even in the lineup."

"Because Finn is friends with literally everybody," Mia grins.

She can't fight back the smile spreading across her face. It's a relatively small festival, but it's still a big deal, and potentially the biggest audience they've ever played to. Her vision blurs as she blinks back hot tears. They'll be playing on Halloween night, just a month away. "Oh my God."

"I know," Mia beams. She inhales and grits her teeth before speaking again. "So, we have to charge ahead with the second album and get it out there as soon as possible. If not the whole album then we have to at least get a couple of singles out. They want us to play a six-song set, so I'm thinking four from the first album, and two from the second."

Finn nods slowly, his eyes focusing intently on the gaudy hotel carpet. "I called the guy we have auditioning for vocals this morning, he's on his way right now. We need to work on the duets. I think they're our best bet."

Jordan exhales sharply, all too aware of the world's spinning. Four weeks to rehearse and record their singles, and prepare for the festival. Hotel guests chatter quietly, clinking cutlery against their plates as they eat, carrying on as though the world hasn't just completely changed.

Overwhelmed, she stands and heads over to the coffee machine in the back of the breakfast hall. It's a lot to take in, so much, she realizes as she fills her cup, her heart hasn't clenched once at the sight of Finn.

She turns back and watches him as she shakes two sugar packets and tears off the tops. He talks with the band's keyboardist, Liz, gesticulating wildly with his big, broad hands.

Nothing.

Not even a flutter. He just… looks like Finn, her friend, familiar and comforting and although still undoubtedly, objectively handsome, she doesn't feel anything romantic toward him.

Thank fuck.

The combination of alcohol, the romantic setting, and seeing her friend so handsome and happy had been a powerful one. Powerful enough for her to act completely out of character, both with Finn *and* Étienne. Cringing, she tips the sugar into the coffee and heads back toward the group.

"Hey man, you made it!" Finn leaps to his feet and bounds over to the dining hall door. He fills the entire frame with his broad figure, towering above whoever he's speaking to.

Jordan slumps into her chair, grateful of the soothing warmth of the cup in her hands. She's so glad her heart finally saw sense about Finn. She's grateful that she can sit with her friends, looking like complete crud in a ratty grey hoodie and leggings, hungover and quaffing gallons of sugary coffee without judgement. She even has a drip of egg yolk down her front. It doesn't matter. It all worked out.

"Vixens," Finn announces proudly, leading a figure toward them. "This is Étienne, he's auditioning for us today."

Jordan's heart empties. Of all the people in all the world. Motherfucker.

Dressed in black jeans which fit tight to his sturdy thighs, and a snug black t-shirt, she's even more attracted to him than she was the night before. Last night his suit jacket skimmed over his short, stocky figure, but dressed in his regular clothes, she can see the shape of him. His chest is broad and full, his stomach soft and round. He's sturdy, husky, and despite her horror at him being there, she can't keep her eyes from him.

It's a fucking injustice when she's the human embodiment of a hangover.

She tries to recoil further back into the darkness of her hood and brings her coffee cup to her mouth, hiding the lower half of her face.

"Thanks for the opportunity," he says, thrusting his hands into his pockets. He bunches his shoulders a little before exhaling loudly and looking up at Finn. "Do we have a room for auditions or…"

"No, we figured you could just sing for us right here and serenade everyone while they're eating breakfast," Finn chuckles.

"Fine by me," Étienne shrugs, completely unphased by Finn's teasing. He seems so calm, so cool, as though he knows he belongs with the group. Cocky bastard. Cocky sexy bastard.

Finn throws his arm around Étienne's shoulders as if the two of them go way back. "I'm kidding. We have a room. They let us book one of the conference rooms last minute."

Étienne smiles and nods, and the shallow undulation of

his chest catches Jordan's attention. Despite his bravado, he's nervous. She would be too. But damn is he good at hiding it.

"You alright, Jordo?" Finn says, stooping a little to peer into her hood.

Her heart jolts as the attention turns to her. She can't hide forever. If Étienne joins them, sooner or later he'll find out who she is, and the longer she leaves it, the more awkward it will be. She sips her coffee and sets it down on the table. "Yeah, I'm good."

Recognition flashes across Étienne's face. Cold panic seeps through her body as he looks at her with disdain. Of course, he does. She can't really blame him for that.

⸺

She looks at Étienne as though she can eject him from the room with her glare. Even as the physical embodiment of a hangover, she turns his lungs to iron. Her purple hair is tucked away beneath her hood, and she doesn't have last night's smokey eye makeup, but he'd recognize those soulful hazel eyes anywhere. He'd dreamed of them after all.

But this complicates things a little. It's also ridiculous, to the point of hilarity.

At least now he knows her name, or at least can make an educated guess. Jordan. "Hey."

"Hey," she replies, smoothing down her hair.

"How's it going?"

She quirks her eyebrow and gestures to herself. "Had better days."

Finn's face brightens. "You know each other?"

"We met last night," Étienne says, offering her a smile,

which he hopes is reassuring. He's not about to tell her band-mates she came on to him.

But it doesn't work. Her scowl only deepens, and he knows he has to play it cool but he's on the brink of laughter. What are the chances?

A woman stands, casting a glance at Jordan. She has sapphire blue braided hair, dark brown skin, and a warm, welcoming smile. "I'm Mia, by the way. I'm the vocalist, so I need to know that our voices will work together. Are you ready?" She gestures toward the dining hall door with red-taloned hands.

Reality crashes down on top of him. Étienne's amusement shatters, and the nerves almost floor him. A fragile flicker of hope that only Finn and Mia will judge the audition glimmers in the back of his mind, but the light is extinguished as the rest of the band stands. The musicians' eyes fix him in place, watching, waiting expectantly. Only Jordan hangs back a little, patently avoiding him.

"Yeah… yeah," he nods, trying to reassure himself more than any of them. "Let's do this."

They file out of the dining room, Mia and Finn leading the way, and Étienne bringing up the rear. His heart pounds to the beat of their footsteps as they follow a long, warmly lit corridor, past open doors leading to conference rooms and rec areas. He scolds himself for leaving his water bottle in the car.

A grey shape moves in the corner of his vision and he knows at once who it is. Jordan falls into step beside him, her hood down now, and her lavender hair pulled back into a ponytail. Her skin is pale, but her jaw is blotchy and vibrant pink, a blush which doesn't reach her cheeks. Without her heels, she's almost exactly the same height as him.

"I'm sorry," she says quietly, glancing toward him. "I was awful last night."

"You weren't," he assures her.

"I was."

"You were mildly inconsiderate at worst. But I get it. Weddings are stressful, and there was alcohol and a lot of emotions running rampant."

"Still, you didn't deserve to be spoken to that way. I'm sorry." She glances down her chest. There's something pale and crusty stuck to the front of her hoodie, as if she's tried to get it off with her fingernails. "I'm absolutely mortified."

"Are you okay with me auditioning?"

"Yeah. Absolutely."

He nods, simultaneously relieved at her answer and annoyed she didn't give him an out. No matter how embarrassed she might be about last night, at least she doesn't have to sing for him. Fear prickles along his spine as Finn and Mia file off into a room to the right side of the corridor. The rest of the band follow.

Fuck, he can't. He can't do this. Mia is classically trained, an absolute powerhouse of a vocalist and he's pretty sure he's forgotten everything that twenty-five years of practice have ever taught him.

"Are you okay?" Jordan asks beside him.

Hot shame rolls across his face as he realizes they're standing still in the middle of the corridor. He's frozen, his heart pounding like that of a cornered rabbit, his guts tying themselves in knots. His dream of being a musician is hanging by a fraying thread and these are the people at the top of the mountain offering a safety rope. But if he grabs it, he could unbalance them all. One member of the band already feels awkward just being around him.

He could cut his losses now. Go home with at least a shred of pride and scour the internet for musicians searching for singers and try to form a band. Start from scratch playing bars and open mics. His chest aches. There's so little air in the corridor. It was absurd to even think he could be part of a band like Vixen's Wail. He's a wedding singer, not a vocalist in a metal band. It's ridiculous, absolutely—

"Hey," Jordan steps in front of him and reaches out to press her hand around the curve of his forearm. Her palm is cool and dry against his burning skin. "It's okay. Just breathe."

Breathing hurts,, as though he's inhaled broken glass.

"Étienne?"

He raises his eyes to meet hers, dark hazel and filled with concern. She breathes slowly, pulling the air in through her nose, before pursing her lips to exhale. He follows her lead, feeling absurd, telling himself he's only faking the absolute terror and the tight bind around his chest. This isn't genuine panic. It can't be. Étienne doesn't panic.

Nevertheless, she keeps on guiding him, showing him there is air to breathe, filling her lungs just a step ahead of him. And all the while she keeps her hand on his forearm, grounding him. The bind fades, and the world beyond them comes into focus.

Anxiety gives way to embarrassment. He averts his eyes and clears his throat. "I'm okay."

She pulls back her hand, as though his skin burns her and curls her fingers into her palm. "Do you want me to tell them you need a minute? I'm sure they wouldn't mind rescheduling if you need to."

He shakes his head and frowns, almost insulted by the

idea. This isn't him. He's never afraid of auditions or singing. He's been on stage since he was ten years old.

Even with her hand withdrawn, he can still feel the coolness of her touch pressed into his skin. He tries to rub away the sensation, ashamed that he lost his nerve. "I'm fine."

"Okay. Just take all the time you need." Her eyes flicker briefly to the warm, tingling patch on his arm, before she turns on her heel, leading the way toward the room.

As she walks away, he presses his hand over the impression of her touch, as though he can somehow seal it, keep it on his skin forever. With a start he dismisses the thought. He is not doing this. He knows next to nothing about her, and the best-case scenario is that they'll be working together. The worst is that he's about to humiliate himself in front of her.

No. Not going to happen.

And yet his stomach flops a little as she glances over her shoulder to check if he's following before disappearing through the doorway.

He'd better get it over with, he tells himself as he rotates his shoulders and tries to psych himself up. One way or the other, he's destined to make a fool of himself.

FIVE

Jordan sits beside Mia, flexing her fingers as the warmth of Étienne's skin haunts her. She feels more than a little guilty about paying attention to the firm muscles of his forearms while he was panicking, but as soon as she had touched him her mind split into two; one half intent on protecting him, and the other fanning the flames of a primal heat.

"Are we good?" Mia mutters without looking up from her phone.

Jordan clenches her fist and tucks it beneath her other arm. "Yeah."

"Did you and this guy…?"

"No." Her answer is firm and mostly guilt-free. Though she doesn't admit it wasn't through lack of trying.

Mia sets her phone on her lap and smiles. "Alright. But you know we vote on this as a band. All of us have to be in agreement. If this is in any way making you uncomfortable, speak up."

She appreciates the sentiment, but if anyone is uncomfortable it's Étienne. He's still out in the corridor. Hell, he could be halfway back to the parking lot by now, fleeing for his life.

Her fears are assuaged as he walks through the door, closing it behind him. She finds herself rooting for him so damned hard as he struts to the center of the room and gives a breathless chuckle. This is not something she could ever do in a thousand years, and as far as she's concerned, his courage is monumental.

"You need a backing track?" Finn asks, holding up his phone and a small black Bluetooth speaker.

Étienne shakes his head and brings his hands to his face in a prayer position, touching the edges of his index fingers to his lips. He rocks back and forth a little, as if preparing to take a running leap off a cliff.

It's Jordan's turn to seize up and hold her breath. She's anxious for him, simultaneously desperate for him to succeed, and half hoping he'll be a bad fit for the band, and she'll never have to see him again.

Because how can she work like this?

Every moment they share the same space is torment. No matter how hard she scolds herself or tries to focus on literally anything else, she's drawn to him, pulled by some imaginary force. It's an intensity she has felt only once before, and that terrifies her.

But then Étienne screws his eyes shut, fills his lungs, and begins to sing. The back of her neck prickles, at the raw, heart-shattering sound, a soul laid bare for her to weigh and measure. It's a song she hasn't heard before, with deep, growling lows, and soaring highs, showing the full extent of his impressive range. It's beautiful. Devastating.

And when he gets to the chorus, the air crackles around

her and her soul leaves her. The power of each note pulls it straight from her body. Her nerves fire, spreading coiling, tingling tendrils beneath the surface of her skin, sending shivers up the back of her neck and down her arms.

Beside her, Mia sits, eyes closed, chin dipped as she listens. Finn leans sideways against the wall, lips parted as he stares at the carpet. The rest of the band watch Étienne closely, exchanging covert glances and grinning. They're going to say yes, they have to. Étienne is incredible.

Goosebumps spread across Jordan's skin and she folds her arms over herself as the tingle spreads to her chest. Beneath the thick grey fabric of her hoodie, her nipples grow tight. Working with him is going to be torture, she can tell. Her body wants him, *craves him*, but she can't ever make him uncomfortable again. He told her no, and that's the end of it.

When the song ends, and the band applaud, Étienne keeps his eyes closed as he rubs his forehead and pushes out a breath. And when those heavy grey eyes open, they focus straight onto her, scouring her face. Her heart skips.

She wants to tell him he was incredible, but she clings to the words. They're the only thing he left her with after shattering her heart with his song.

The rest of the band laugh, forcing out labored breaths, as though the sound had barricaded their throats too. Everyone in the room is speechless.

It's Finn who puts their thoughts into words. "That was fucking sexy, my dude."

They all laugh, because ever the poet, Finn sums it up perfectly. Everything about Étienne is sexy. Despite her protests, despite telling herself she shouldn't think it, she so desperately wants him.

"It was gorgeous," Mia chuckles, uncrossing her legs to

lean forward. She braces her elbows on her thighs and rests her chin on her fists. "Do you mind if we sing something together? See how that sounds?"

"Sure," Étienne nods. He's a little out of breath from the song, his forehead glistening as he sweeps back his hair.

Jordan's mind races as Mia jumps to her feet and she and Étienne figure out a song to sing. It's clear they have slightly different tastes in music, and altogether different repertoires. Perhaps he won't fit after all. But frustratingly, after a few minutes of deliberation they reach an agreement.

She's so engrossed in Mia and Étienne's conversation, she doesn't notice Finn until he's already sinking into the empty seat beside her, his arms folded over his broad chest. Last night, his closeness would've sent her spiraling, but today, she's calmed by the familiarity of his presence. He leans in close, pressing his tattooed arm to hers before he whispers, "What do you think?"

Honestly, she thinks that Étienne is the most handsome man she's ever seen. That working with him on these songs is going to turn her to a puddle.

"He's pretty good." She shrugs to give off an air of nonchalance. "Definitely worth considering. But I also think you should be spending today with your wife."

Finn fixes her in an incredulous stare before a grin breaks his outraged veneer. "I will be, once we're finished up here. Actually, I sent her to the spa for the morning, so she's happy."

"Ooh," Jordan whispers playfully, narrowing her eyes. "Nice."

He sits back, proud and beaming. "I'm a good husband."

"Good."

This is how it should be, how it always is. No awkwardness between them, no misguided crushes. Vixens Wail are her family, or, better than. Letting someone new into that means a lot.

"Hey," she begins, but the apology on behalf of her foolish heart snags on the tip of her tongue. She can't let Finn ever know how she felt. Not ever. So instead, she tells him the truth. "I'm really happy for you. Both of you."

Finn's eyes crease as he smiles. "Thanks."

Étienne and Mia begin to sing together, and although their sounds are so wildly different, it works. Mia's rich, pitch-perfect voice, intertwining with Étienne's raw and untrained talent. An angel and a demon serenading each other, and pulling the rest of the world into love with them.

"Holy shit," Finn whispers. "This is going to be big."

Jordan folds her arms over her chest again, fighting back the shivers their voices send across her skin. He's right.

When the song is over, Étienne is sent to wait in an adjacent meeting room while the band deliberates the outcome.

"I think I'm in love with him," Finn laughs, raking his fingers through his hair. "There's a big heart and a lot of sound in that little dude."

"I'm on board," Mia says, sitting back in her chair and tapping her fingernails on the wooden arm. She fixes her gaze on Jordan, and arches an eyebrow, silently asking if everything is alright. "So long as the rest of you are comfortable with him being here."

Mia's meaning is clear.

É tienne sits alone in a conference room, at the head of a large oval table. His breath is steadier since the audition, but his heart still races. In the next room over, the band are debating his fate.

At least he can say he gave it his all.

All he can do is sit and wait, and hope they weren't deterred by him closing his eyes throughout the performance, because if he'd made eye contact with them, he knows he would have frozen. But the look on Jordan's face afterwards was every bit as silencing. She looked…afraid. Afraid of him.

Last night he'd thought she was staring at Finn. It was hard not to notice, and perhaps he shouldn't have said anything, but he didn't want to be used as the stick stirring already muddied waters. Today, he's not so sure. Had he known they work together, that they make music together, he wouldn't have thought it strange that she kept watching him.

He sits back and tilts his face to the ceiling, rubbing his eyes until he sees spots. The tangled mess of thoughts only gets knots tighter the more he pays attention to it. She'd wanted him last night, but not for *him*. Just sex. She didn't even give him her name, and hadn't wanted him to find her, and yet here he is, afraid to sing to her in case he falls for her.

He needs to snap out of it.

Étienne has always fallen hard, too fast, too desperately. It wasn't until his mid-twenties he finally began to accept himself for who he is, that he was only ever going to fulfill two thirds of the tall, dark, and handsome trinity. But before that he'd latched onto any attention he could get, and old habits die hard.

"Hey?"

The sound of her voice damn near stops his heart as he

bolts upright and pushes his chair back to stand. Jordan stands in the doorway, her lips pressed together into a hard line. It's bad news. He knows it.

"Hey." His throat is rough, dry. He can *see* the water bottle in his car, nestled in the cupholder.

She steps into the room and closes the door behind her, before walking to the opposite end of the oval table. "I'm sorry this is weird."

"It's not," he lies.

He eyes the closed door. If they need privacy, it could be really bad. His mind flings itself headlong into baseless conclusions. She's going to tell him they decided he was so bad, he should never sing again, he knows it.

"I want to ask you if you're okay with it," she begins. "Given… what happened last night. I know we didn't get off to a good start."

"I thought we did. I thought it was a great start. It was the part after that got a little rocky."

She presses her lips together and nods. "Yeah. But what I'm asking, is now that you know I'm in the band, would you be comfortable working with us?"

His heart lifts a little, buoyed by hope. "Of course."

She smiles, a sweet smile of relief, and walks toward him, her hand held out for him to shake.

"Can we start over?" she asks. "I'm Jordan."

"I'm still Étienne." He stands and accepts her offered hand, giving it a firm shake. Her eyes meet his, and a tingle rolls through his body. "So, does this mean I got the gig?"

"How could we say no?" She beams. "You were incredible."

Heat rises up his neck, flushing his jaw. Fortunately, and intentionally, his beard hides most of his blushes, which come all too often. He tries to stay cool, tries to keep from grinning by sinking his teeth into his lower lip.

Jordan's breath catches in her throat before she looks away and pulls her hand back from his. "Do you want to head back to the other room? We can figure out rehearsals with the rest of the band."

"Yeah. Yeah. Cool."

He's lightheaded as he follows her, half convinced she's going to turn around and tell him it was all a joke. It's all too good to be true, and when she does turn, his heart plummets.

"Uh." She winces, hiding her hands inside the sleeves of her hoodie. "Listen. Just to get this out in the open… I know I was the pushy one last night, but from here on out we're just purely professional, okay? We work together."

"Okay. Yeah. That's totally fine."

"Thank you. And I'm so sorry again for last night. I was…" She laughs, looking away from him. "God, I was so drunk."

It was pretty hard to miss, but he doesn't want to embarrass her. Is he relieved or disappointed? Perhaps a little of both.

The band greet him like an old friend, standing to hug him, to congratulate him on a killer audition. Finn crushes Étienne in his big, strong arms, pummeling his back with effusive fists.

And all the while Jordan stands on the sidelines, eyes averted, hands tucked up inside the cuffs of her hoodie, a clear sign she doesn't want any part of this boisterous affection.

"Hold on, back up," Mia says clearly, breaking apart the celebration. "Before we get too carried away, we need to let

Étienne know what's going on and why we had to rush the audition."

The rest of the band step back, all watching him intently with excited smiles on their faces. All except one.

Mia pulls in a breath and places her hands on her hips, drumming her red fingernails on the waistband of her jeans.

Étienne waits as she purses her lips together and nods, thinking of the best way to drop whatever news she's holding onto.

"So," she says at last, casting a wry smile at Finn before looking back at him. "How would you feel about getting on stage and headlining with us at Ghoulfest in four weeks?"

As the world lurches around him and a mixture of fear and excitement courses through his body, his eyes trail back to Jordan. She's watching him but he can't read the expression on her face. Is she rooting for him, wanting him to say yes, or is she willing him to say no, to take this final get-out-of-jail free card?

Perhaps she's feeling a bit of both too?

"What do you think?" Finn asks beside him. "It's going to be a tight schedule, but if we pull it off, this could be huge for us and for you."

At last, Jordan's eyes meet his and her lips part as she inhales. Just the sight of her sends tingles shooting through his body. Nothing this big has ever come his way but working with her is going to be agony. He doesn't dare hope that the suffering won't be one-sided.

Perhaps she was only being kind by welcoming him into the band. But then her expression softens and a reassuring smile graces her lips.

"I'm in," he says, his nervousness tightening a coil in the pit of his stomach. "When do we start?"

Six

A week later the band is back on a rehearsal schedule and Finn is home from his short and sweet honeymoon. As Jordan pulls up outside their rehearsal space—an old, repurposed factory, she turns the engine off and sits in silence. A week has passed since that day at the hotel. She'd like to say she's over Étienne just as quickly as she was over Finn, but that would be a lie.

Closing her eyes, she prays he somehow lost his looks and swagger since she saw him last, and now has all the sexuality of an unseasoned rice cake.

But she doubts it.

The intensity of her attraction scares her. It was like this with Danny all those years ago.

She tenses at just the thought of his name.

Before Danny she had never truly been afraid of another person. Her entire life, she had been surrounded by gentle guys, her sweet dad, her dorky older brother, and Finn who was more teddy bear than grizzly. Danny never laid a finger on her, but the hate in his eyes, the way he hissed every vile word between his teeth when they fought, it scared her. Like he was holding back.

He never raised his hand to her, but he left a mark all the same.

Even after he was gone, the war continued. The name Vixen's Wail was mud at every venue. He did everything he could to break the band apart, and when that didn't work, he slashed tires, smashed windows, and spray-painted Jordan's home with every despicable name he could think of for her. Not only had she apparently broken his heart by refusing to accept he needed to sleep with other women, but she had cost him his future. The remaining Vixens taught her that wasn't true.

So, no, even if Étienne does seem kind and gentle, even if they do seem to get along well, she won't risk another relationship with a band member. She won't risk the band for another guy. Never again.

She has to retain control.

The sound of a sputtering engine catches her attention. A small blue hatchback trundles and rattles down the road toward her, leaving a cloud of black smoke in its wake. Jordan winces as the car pulls into a parking spot and the brakes squeal.

"Jeez," she whispers. "What a deathtrap."

Probably some teenager starting his first band. She remembers all too well the rust buckets various members of Vixen's Wail drove when they first began playing together. Not to mention that year she rode a bicycle to practice every day with a cello strapped to her back.

Until Finn met Beth, they'd had to make do with rehearsing in whatever cramped space they could find. Often it was one of their living rooms or basements and would result in complaints from their neighbors.

Jordan smiles at the memory. How far they've come. She silently hopes that this kid in the blue hatchback will make it too.

But it isn't a kid. Not at all. When Étienne gets out of the car her heart just about stops. Good lord, that man can fill out a pair of jeans.

His simple black t-shirt strains over his compact frame, highlighting every hill and valley of his shape. Right away the sight of him ties her stomach in knots.

"Shit," she whispers.

He's just Étienne she tells herself, just her bandmate. Good old Étienne on his way to practice. On his way to give her goosebumps with his powerful voice, and to grunt and gasp between bursts of songs.

The hairs on her arms stand on end at the thought of it.

In what universe is this remotely fair? The image of him at the wedding, deliberately stepping behind his chair as if he were afraid that she would pounce on him haunts her. Hot shame rolls across her face.

Even if they could move past that, even if she could get over their embarrassment, she refuses to pursue him. He's part of the band now, a Vixen. No matter what, she can't risk that. She isn't about to give it all up for a short king with a serious case of big dick energy, even if he is the most absurdly handsome man she's ever seen.

She looks back up, and almost jumps out of her skin. Étienne is looking over at her, cautiously raising a hand in greeting as he squints to make sure it's her. Well, she has to get it over with at some point.

Whispering one last "shit" for good measure, she opens the door and climbs out of the car. "Hi!" she calls brightly.

"How's it going?"

Her heart beats harder as he walks over. No, he *struts* over. It isn't deliberate or forced, just the gait of a natural born showman who happens to be hot as Hades' toaster oven.

"Ah…Not bad." She opens the trunk of her car and pulls out her cello from its bed of pillows and blankets. Catching his scent on the breeze her mouth dries out. He smells like cool, fresh cologne. "You?"

He chuckles a little and glances over his shoulder at his beat-up car. "Eh. It's been a day."

"That's better than bad though?"

He smiles and damn near throws her into cardiac arrest. "You're pink."

Bringing a hand to her burning cheeks, embarrassment tightens her chest. He has to know she's still hot for him, her face is practically searing off her fingertips. "Oh no… I had the heater on in the car and—"

"No, I mean your hair," he laughs. "You were purple before, now you're pink."

This fucker. There's no way he doesn't know what he's doing. She brings a hand to the top of her head and smooths down her ponytail. She'd dyed it again a few days ago. "Oh, yeah."

She slams down the trunk and steps out from behind the car. His eyes immediately fall to the cello case in her hand.

"Do you need help with it?"

Jordan shakes her head. "Thanks though."

"My pleasure."

That word on his full lips rolls through her body turning

her legs to jelly. He lets her lead the way into the factory, past the perpetually unmanned reception desk and up four flights of stairs.

"I've never been here before," he says, slightly out of breath.

Jordan tries her hardest not to sound like she's dying after the climb. "It's a pretty new place. It was just abandoned forever until it was bought and turned into an arts center and they started hiring it out for rehearsals. Finn's wife has something to do with it. Which is a good thing because I don't think any of us have a single neighbor who we haven't pissed off."

Étienne chuckles. "Yeah, I've had my fair share of noise complaints."

"Oh, I doubt that. Your neighbors are lucky they get to hear you sing…" she trails off, inwardly scolding herself for gushing.

But Étienne doesn't seem to mind. He smiles, pressing his teeth into his lower lip. "I love your sound by the way."

"The band?"

"No. Well, yes…but I mean *your* sound. Your cello."

She stops outside the room they have booked and turns to face him fully. Now he's blushing. It's barely visible over the shadow of his beard, but it's there, and the sight of his pink cheeks sends signals straight between her thighs.

It's impossible. She still wants him. No matter how hard she tries to push the desire away, she does. In that moment she wants to slam into him, pin him against the wall and suck that pouty lower lip. Fuck everything she thought she knew about herself and the world. She wants him.

They're almost the exact same height, their bodies aligned so they could press against each other, feeling every curve.

The tingles between her thighs turn to full-blown pulses as she imagines the sounds he'd make when he's turned on.

It scares her.

He gives a small breathless laugh and his grey eyes meet hers. "When you play it gives me goosebumps."

J ordan is every bit as beautiful as he remembers, and he has to remind himself constantly, she's completely off limits. She's his bandmate now, and he won't do anything to jeopardize his time with Vixen's Wail, even if she does make his stomach turn somersaults.

Her eyes scour his face, studying every feature as his compliment hovers in the air above them. He swears her breath catches in her throat, swears he sees color rise in her cheeks, but he can't be sure.

"Come on," she mutters. "We're late already."

Étienne follows obediently, a well-trained puppy at her heels as she opens the door and the quiet corridor is flooded with sound.

Stepping across the threshold they enter the rehearsal room. Grey waffle-textured soundproof padding covers the walls and ceiling of the room, which is packed with Vixens. The band is arranged in a circle, all facing each other as they work together on a section of the song.

He'd known Finn's drums would be loud, but he wasn't prepared for the earthshaking thunder. His old band played pop and mellow, classic rock. Standing in a room with a metal drummer with as much power as Finn has in his arms, is like standing in the center of a storm.

"Hi Jordo! Hey, Baby Bear!" the drummer calls as he

thrashes his sticks against a cymbal. "How's it going?"

Ears already ringing, Étienne tries to avert his eyes from Jordan as she picks her way over cables and boxes to the side of the room. There's an empty seat waiting for her next to Mia. The only other space is the opposite side of the circle, between Nic, the band's violinist, and Finn.

"How's it going?" Étienne almost has to scream above the racket as he finds his spot. From his position in the circle, he and Mia can sing directly to each other, which works well for their duet. But it also means he's facing Jordan.

He tries not to watch as she takes her bow from the case and begins to twist the end, tightening the white horsehair. Her movements are almost ritualistic, and the care she takes with the precious—and no doubt expensive—instrument sends a surge of affection rushing through his chest. He clears his throat and turns to Finn. "How was your honeymoon?"

"Awesome," Finn grins. "Short but, you know… every day is awesome with her. Life has been one big honeymoon since we met."

"Adorable!" Mia declares, clapping her hands together. Her fingernails are filed sharp and painted crimson. She wrinkles her nose at Finn. "You two are too cute. You kill me."

Étienne chuckles and adjusts the microphone in front of him, bringing it down a couple of inches. For a moment he allows himself to imagine a life like Finn's; playing music for a living, a car which actually works, married to the love of his life. The guy has everything. It kind of sucks he's so likeable. It makes it hard to be bitter.

As he tightens the screws on the mic stand, he can't help as Jordan lifts her enormous black wood cello from her case, positions it between her knees, and begins to tune it.

A pulse in the base of his belly makes his breath catch. Heat crawls up his neck, flushing his cheeks and drying out his throat as he tries not to look. Tries and fails.

It's so unlike him. He's usually Mr. Cool, but right now, he'd trade his soul just to switch places with that lump of wood, to kneel between her feet and pay homage to every curve and dimple on her body. He would do whatever she asked of him, whatever she demanded—

"Étienne?" Mia says loud and sharp, as though she's tired of saying it. How long has she been calling him?

He snaps to attention and tries to sound innocent. "Hm?"

"You ready?"

Oh god. The whole band is staring at him, waiting for him to stop drooling over the cellist and start singing. "Sorry, I was miles away."

Mia nods. "Yeah. Did you practice the song I sent during the week? *Bloodlust Beautiful?*"

"Yeah." Practice is an understatement. The song is drilled into his memory—and probably that of his neighbors too. He's sung it day and night, refusing to make a fool of himself in front of Vixen's Wail. Hell, he's dreamed of it.

"Good." Mia puts her hands around the head of her microphone and gives a sharp nod to Finn. "Let's do it."

Finn rhythmically beats his sticks together four times, and the band begins to play. Étienne can only stand there in awe at the precision, the way they work together, the chemistry between them. Even their positions in the circle are meticulously planned, he realizes. Finn faces Tamika the bassist as the pair keep rhythm, Anya the guitarist and Liz on keyboards face each other as they weave their melodies. Then there's the strings section, Jordan on cello and Nic the violinist work from opposite ends. He and Mia complete the circle.

And they aren't just playing the song, they're *living* it. Every one of them is living and breathing the notes, the melody, the lyrics.

But not him.

It's as though he's running full-throttle toward the end of a diving board, only to falter and grip the rails at the final second. And now he can't let go. As Mia's flawless verse ends, his cue to sing comes and goes. He's frozen.

The music peters out, and hot shame rolls across his face. His first rehearsal, and he's already screwing up spectacularly. His chest tightens as disappointed glares from the rest of the band burn into him. "Ah, fuck."

"It's alright, dude," Finn assures him as he wipes his shining brow on the crook of his elbow. "We can go again."

Étienne drags his hands over his eyes, before screwing them shut and opening them, desperate to wake up from this nightmare, desperate to be anyone else other than the fuckup standing there with those professional musicians watching him. But it doesn't work. He's still there, still him. He nods. "Okay, let's go."

Mortified is an understatement. It's an old building, so with any luck it could just collapse on top of him and bury him beneath the rubble. Anything would be preferable to this. He can't even look at Jordan right now.

Finn smacks his sticks together four times, counting the band in, and just as before they launch into the song.

Closing his eyes, Étienne listens to Mia, to the power and beauty of her voice. The world sways around him as he fights for breath, gulping in the stifling air. There are no windows in the rehearsal room, just the noise, the heat, the band he has somehow tricked into letting him join them. There's an imposter among them and they're moments from discovering him.

He sees his cue coming a mile off and does nothing as it passes him by.

The music stops, and he doesn't dare open his eyes. Mia's mic amplifies her frustrated sigh.

"Dude, are you okay?" Finn asks.

But Étienne can't answer. Even if he could put his shame into words, he can't draw breath to speak it. As he turns and hurries out of the rehearsal room, letting the door slam behind him, he knows he can't ever show his face in front of Vixen's Wail again.

It takes Jordan a second to get out from under her cello, and in that time, Étienne has already bolted out the door.

"Great," Mia sighs, turning her back on the mic. "We've got a runner."

"He's just nervous," Finn shrugs, making his way across the room.

"We've got four weeks, Finn. We can't screw this up."

"We'll bring him back." Jordan is only a step ahead of the drummer as they head out of the door and down the empty hallway.

"Shit," Finn hisses as they begin their search.

There are doors and winding corridors all throughout the building, but it's unlikely Étienne will be in any of them. Instead, Jordan heads for the stairs.

"I bet he's heading to his car." She's vaguely aware Finn is looking at her, grinning as they head to the end of the hall. "What?"

"You're worried about him," he says.

"Obviously."

The drummer hums thoughtfully.

Finn is considerably taller than her, and he pulls ahead as they race down the stairs and out of the building. The sky is grey and heavy, and though it hasn't started raining yet, the air is cold and damp against Jordan's skin. The repetitive whirr of a struggling engine leads them to Étienne's blue hatchback.

Jordan jogs the last few steps, relieved the singer hasn't gotten away completely, but wondering where exactly they go from here. "Étienne can we talk?"

In place of an answer Étienne turns the engine again, staring straight ahead and sitting completely still. He won't look at her. The engine sputters. The car remains motionless as the knuckles of his left hand turn deathly white on the steering wheel.

"Hey dude," Finn says gently beside Jordan. "Talk to us, we can work this out."

Étienne's shoulders deflate and he turns to face them. His door clicks open but he remains seated. He holds it open just a crack and says quietly, "The window won't open either."

"It's all good," Finn assures him.

Jordan's pulse races as she tries to figure out what to say. If she goes about it the wrong way and he bolts again it could be for good. "You okay?"

A muscle in his cheek flexes at the sound of her voice. "No. I fucked up."

"We've all frozen at some point or another—"

"Not me." The sharp edge to his voice takes her back, as

though the very thought of it is an insult. "I've been singing in front of audiences since I was a kid. I don't freeze up." He unbuckles his seatbelt and stands, closing the door and leaning back against it. "I don't know what's happening to me."

Jordan's throat tightens. She wants to hug him, to let him know everything is okay and he can try as many times as he needs to. There have been times where even Mia has missed her cue to come in, or Finn has gone completely off rhythm. They're good but they're not perfect. They're human.

But as she tries to scrape together enough courage to offer him comfort, Finn steps in and smothers Étienne in an embrace. "It happens to the best of us, Baby Bear."

Jordan fights back a smile as Étienne gently pats Finn's back. His arms and hands are the only parts of him still visible beneath the hulking mountain of drummer.

Étienne's voice is muffled as he speaks. "I can't show my face in there again."

"Yes, you can." Finn chuckles. "You have to. Everyone in the band is smitten with your pretty face. Aren't we, Jord?"

She freezes. Smitten is an understatement, but she'll die before she admits it again. Instead, she hides behind a barricade of deadpan humor. "He's alright, I guess. Maybe a seven out of ten?"

The men break their embrace and glare at her.

She shrugs, "I mean, I'd say a six, but since you're having a bad day, I'm feeling charitable."

"I'm easily a ten," Étienne retorts. His expression is flint, but as he looks into her eyes the corner of his mouth curves into the suggestion of a smile.

He knows she agrees, she's sure, but she'll take the hit to her dignity if it helps him feel better.

"Ignore her, you're at least a twelve," Finn sighs, rolling his eyes. "But the point still stands. There's not a single member of the band who hasn't had a bad day or froze or played off key. It happens."

Étienne nods and looks down at his shoes. "On their first day though?"

"Oh God, we were atrocious," Finn chuckles.

Memories of the band's first practice draw a smile from Jordan. Every one of them was a sloppy mess that day, an enthusiastic, off-key, off-beat mess, and they had never felt more elated in their lives. They hadn't known the catastrophes that awaited them. They were oblivious to the desolate lows and life-affirming highs to come.

"I'm going to head inside and let Mia know you're coming back up," Finn smiles, clapping Étienne on the shoulder. "Jord, will stay out here with you until you're ready to come back in, okay?"

Jordan nods, but she silently curses the drummer as he strolls away, leaving her and Étienne alone in the parking lot. She steps back a pace, putting a safe distance between them as he stands with his back against the door of his car, staring at the asphalt.

When Finn disappears inside Étienne throws back his head and sighs, "Fuck."

If it was anyone else, she would make a "well I'm game if you are" joke, but not with him. So she stands, silent, waiting for the right words to come to her.

"Well?" Étienne says. He's looking at her expectantly. "How badly did I embarrass myself up there?"

She puffs a breath out and arches an eyebrow. "I've seen worse."

"Oh, yeah?"

She nods slowly, "Yeah. You ever been so nervous before a gig that you puked into a brand-new five-hundred-dollar fiberglass cello case?"

"That's… gross." Étienne wrinkles his nose and the corners of his mouth turn down in disgust.

"Yup. I'd been stress-eating pizza backstage too. Just cramming down slices until we were called out onto stage. There was a lot of pepperoni, and a lot of very queasy, extremely pissed off people in the audience."

And just like that, the tension over them lifts. He chuckles, his smile bright and almost grateful. "Did you have to get a new one?"

"Are you kidding me? It was five hundred dollars. No, I carry my puke case with pride."

This time when his nose wrinkles, it's because he's laughing, and it's just about the sweetest thing she's ever seen. As handsome and suave as he can be, he has one hell of an adorably dorky laugh.

Ah, fuck. What she wouldn't give to sit on that face.

He shakes his head and chuckles. "I suppose I should be grateful I didn't throw up."

"We all should," she nods. "It's a small room with no ventilation."

Their laughter dies down, fading to fond smiles as their eyes meet. And then their smiles fade too. Flutters roll through her stomach as his gaze drops lower. To her mouth.

His breath catches breaking the weight of the air between them. "We'd better go inside."

"Yeah." She's almost relieved as he pushes off from the car door and starts walking back toward the factory. Just a moment, just a heartbeat longer, and she would have risked it all for those lips.

SEVEN

He can't figure Jordan out. One moment her eyes are locked with his, gazing deep into his soul, the next she can't even look at him. When he first met her, she was a bombshell wrapped in green velvet, and now she's in ripped jeans and an old t-shirt, telling him gross stories to make him laugh, and he's hopelessly endeared to both versions of her.

Maybe this is a good thing, Étienne tells himself as he holds the factory's front door open for her. It's good to get to know the less-sexy things about her so he can move on from this crush and just be her friend. He'd like that, he really would.

But as she starts to climb the staircase a few steps ahead of him, putting her round ass directly at eye-level, he forgets his performance anxiety.

"How do you feel?" she asks, casting a glance over her shoulder.

Honestly, he's a wiggle away from forgetting his own name. "Pretty good." He forces himself to look away and think of something else. Something other than Jordan or singing.

Of course, he fails at both.

By the time they get back to the rehearsal room his chest is tight and nervous energy hums through his body. He's scared and more than a little turned on, and when Jordan stops just before opening the door, he almost crashes into her.

"Hey," she spins around to face him, one hand on the door handle. He loves that they're the same height, that they're always at eye-level. "Listen, I know this is intimidating, performing in front of us, but you're incredible. Really. Your voice is just…it's…" she trails off and exhales hard, as though she can't find the words to express herself. She looks up to the ceiling, smiling, and shakes her head. "I know you're going to kill it. Your voice is incredible. You're amazing."

A knot in his chest tightens as her eyes dart over his features, assessing every inch of his face before creasing with her smile.

"Thanks." He barely makes a sound as he speaks.

"Deep breaths," she reminds him before opening the door.

The rehearsal room is shrouded in silence, heavy and oppressive like the air before a storm. The bandmates who can bear to make eye contact smile at him tentatively, as if they're afraid to make too much noise in case he spooks and runs away again.

"I'm sorry," Étienne says as he makes his way back to his spot in the circle. He looks up just in time to see Finn cast a wry smile at Jordan.

"It's alright," Mia says gently, her hands on her hips as she waits for him to get ready. "You good?"

"I'm good."

He isn't. Not by a long shot, but as Jordan sits and prepares to play again, her words echo through his mind.

Jordan believes in him.

It's only the third time they've met but she's seen him at highs and lows already. She's seen him sipping cocktails after being stood-up at the wedding, she's seen him panic and freeze twice, and she's heard him open his heart and sing like his life depends on it, because it does. He sings. It's who he is. And she believes in him.

"Alright," Finn says. "Let's do this. *Bloodlust.* From the top."

The music starts and he can't keep his eyes off Jordan. She plays passionately, eyes closed, ear tilted toward the sound, her eyebrows knit together in concentration. She's so beautiful. Not just physically, but her heart. It's laid bare when she plays, and he adores it.

As Mia's verse comes to an end, Jordan opens her eyes and looks at him, and the spark in his chest ignites. He grips the microphone and he sings. He sings to her.

He sings for her.

É tienne sings with raw passion, his knuckles pale as he grips the mic stand. When he fills his lungs, he gasps and moans between the lines, sort of overly suggestive but so goddamn sexy. The whole time Jordan's thighs are kept parted by the cello. She can't even squeeze them together to relieve some of the need building there.

He's magnetic. It's in the passion with which he sings, the beads of sweat which run down the straining sinews of his neck, the thrust of his hips as he loses himself to the music.

By the end of practice, she's a puddle, a trembling, horny wreck. As she loosens the screw at the end of her bow, slackening the horsehair, she tries to steady her breath. She knew he would be incredible, but nothing prepared her for the sounds that this man can make.

It's almost laughable that she thought she could get away with a no-strings-attached fling with Étienne. Even without the fling part, there are definitely strings binding them, and whether it's intentional or not they're tightening around them. It's as worrying as it is exciting, but she knows she needs to step back, for the sake of the band if nothing else. She needs to cut them.

"Hey." His voice at her back straightens her spine.

Her breath catches as she clips her case shut and turns to face him. He's standing in the center of the room, lifting the bottom hem of his shirt to his face as he dabs sweat from his forehead. It's impossible to keep her eyes from the pale flash of his stomach beneath the black cotton of his shirt. His body is soft and thick, dusted with dark hair, and the sight of his bare skin dries her mouth out.

Her fingers flex around the handle of her case. "You were amazing," she smiles, hoping he can't hear the tremble in her voice. "Really."

He drops his shirt back down and flashes her a grin. "I know."

She arches a judgmental eyebrow, but his cockiness only makes her want him more. "Oh, you do?"

"I do, and I want to say thank you. What you said to me before we came back in here really helped."

"Oh." It takes her back. She can barely even remember exactly what she said. It was incoherent and clumsy; despite the fact she had practiced saying it about twenty times as they climbed the stairs. "Well, I'm glad."

His smile broadens as Finn barrels out the door, holding up a finger signaling the band to stay put. He turns back to her and fixes her in that come-to-bed gaze. "Just…Thank you."

A moment later and the drummer returns, followed by his wife, Beth.

Jordan groans as Finn pulls out his phone and hands it off so Beth can take photos.

"Are you serious? Now?" Jordan grumbles.

Finn grins. "We need to make an announcement about the collaboration with Étienne."

Jordan sighs as she sets aside her cello. "Why do you always do this after practice when we're gross and sweaty?"

"We're not gross and sweaty," Mia retorts. "We're sexy and glistening. Get in the photo, Jord."

The band arrange themselves in front of Finn's kit and Jordan reluctantly obeys, standing on the edge of the group beside Étienne.

Pressing her back to the door, Beth grimaces as she holds the phone horizontally. "You're going to have to squish in a little. Little more."

They shuffle together, Jordan's hip pressed to Étienne's, closer and closer, until she's almost overbalancing.

"Little closer," Beth laughs.

"If we get any closer, we'll have our first Vixen orgy," Tamika the bassist cries out in the middle of the pile. "Take the picture."

"Jordan needs to get in a bit more," Beth says, wafting her hand in encouragement.

Jordan grits her teeth. She sure is glad Beth makes Finn happy, but right now she could happily strangle her. Turning her body sideways, she braces herself and presses her front to Étienne's side, draping one arm around the backs of his shoulders.

He smells so good, cologne and sweat and heat, and her body hums with need for him. Her heart skips as he lifts his arm and wraps it around her waist, holding her to him. He's so close she can hear his shallow breaths, feel the waves of warmth coming from his body.

He turns his head, inching toward her. "Close enough?" His voice is quiet and rough-edged. There's a darkness there she hasn't heard before.

And the answer is no.

No, this isn't close enough. She wants him to turn toward her, to press his body against hers and peel off their clothes. She wants to be so close to him she doesn't know where she ends and he begins.

But she can't say it. No matter how much she wants him she can't have him.

She stands transfixed by his eyes like a rabbit caught in steely grey headlights. His lips part just a little, and his fingers tighten at her waist. His breath is warm against her skin. Just an inch closer and their lips will be touching.

The whir of an artificial shutter breaks the spell.

Panicked, Jordan whips her head to face the camera as it clicks and clicks, her breath locked tight in her chest. What-ever the fuck just passed between them, it leaves her shaken and unsteady, her mind unable to focus on anything but the heat of his hand on her waist, and the tingling sensation rolling through her. It should feel wrong, too much too soon. But it doesn't.

A moment later and Beth says, "done." The group disperses, grumbling and rubbing squashed limbs and bruised ribs. Jordan's waist grows cold as Étienne withdraws his hand and turns away to head back over to his spot in the circle.

But the heat beneath the surface of her skin, that takes far longer to fade.

So much for cutting the strings.

"Hey, Finn, you need help taking the drums down to your car?" Étienne tries to keep his voice light and even, but the truth is he's burning from the inside out.

Jordan had been pressed so close to him, soft and warm and just so right.

She doesn't even acknowledge him as she gathers up her cello case and bolts for the door. Fuck. He doesn't know what happened between them, only that it was intense, sexy, and unprofessional as hell.

Finn grins to Beth as they look over the photos on his phone. The couple exchange a look before he leans over and kisses her on the cheek.

"Thanks, Baby Bear, but I'm good," the drummer says at last, turning to face Étienne. "I leave this kit here."

"Is it secure?"

"Normally no, but I have friends in high places."

Beth shakes her head as she laughs and heads over to the door. She reaches for the handle with a paint-smeared hand. "See you tonight."

"I love you," Finn calls. "Thank you for the pictures."

She darts out of the room, calling over her shoulder. "Love you too."

Étienne's chest aches a little as he shoves his hands into the pockets of his jeans. He doesn't even have Jordan's number. He can't text or call her to apologize or figure out what happened. He just has to wait until their next rehearsal in a couple of days.

The band pack up and make their way out of the rehearsal room. The atmosphere among them is buzzing, but Étienne's mind isn't on his performance or how good the duet sounds. It's on her. When he gets out to the parking lot her car is nowhere to be seen.

"You were awesome today," Finn says as they approach Étienne's car. Specks of rain fall from the oppressive grey clouds, and the air has a biting chill to it, but the drummer is dressed as though it's the middle of summer in a flimsy black muscle tank, which barely contains his hulking frame and shows off his tattooed arms. "I'm glad you came back in."

"Me too," Étienne smiles.

It's the truth, even if the rehearsal did get a little... complicated toward the end, he's glad he came back. He might be a long way from making a living from his music, but today felt like a huge first step toward that goal. Perhaps his run of bad luck is over.

When he gets inside the car, he pulls in a deep breath and releases a longing sigh. He can still feel her against him. His fingers still tingle where he touched her waist. Perhaps it was too much. Did she stare at him like that because she couldn't believe his audacity, or because she felt it too? Because for him it wasn't just a spark. It was a detonation.

One by one, the Vixens—his bandmates—drive away.

He turns the key in the ignition, expecting that familiar grating whine from the engine, but to his horror, he's met with silence. "Oh shit."

As he tries again and again his chest hollows. There isn't even a flicker of life from the vehicle. The engine must have completely died during his earlier attempt to escape.

Fortunately, Finn is only just pulling away.

Étienne hurries from his lifeless vehicle and chases Finn's beat-up black van through the parking lot. Thankfully the drummer stops just before he gets out onto the main road.

"You okay, Baby Bear?"

Gripping the glass of the half-open window, Étienne shakes his head, each hard-fought breath tearing through his chest with its claws bared. "My car's dead."

"Aw, shit. Come on in then, I'll get you home," Finn chuckles, leaning over to open the passenger side door. "You have to navigate though."

With a grunt Étienne hops up into the van and buckles his seatbelt. He'll have to deal with the car tomorrow. Maybe. Right now, he can't afford to repair it, but he can't afford not to have a car either.

"You okay?" Finn asks as they stop at a stop sign.

"Yeah, just… turn left here… just money stuff."

Finn follows the direction and grimaces. "I'm sorry, that sucks."

"Yeah." It more than sucks. The weight of it all is crushing, a constant pressure on his chest. "I know how lucky I am to have been able to support myself for so long with the money I make from gigs but… I don't know. I can feel time running out."

"What do you mean?"

It's painful to even admit. Pride latches his lips, but it has been too long since he told anyone. If he doesn't let it out, he won't sleep tonight. The dam bursts and his worries pour. "Rent's due and… with the car and all. Food and bills. I know. I need to find a job."

"Do you need an advance?"

The question throws Étienne off guard. He sits completely still, blinking as the exit they were supposed to take comes and goes. "You'd do that?"

Finn shrugs, "Yeah, of course. You need to get to rehearsals and gigs, so you need your car back. I can't afford to pay you the full amount early but I'm sure I can stretch to the cost of car repairs. I know a guy who can fix it."

Étienne's throat is already tired and a little raw from spending the whole afternoon singing, but the lump there now is agony. His vision blurs as he blinks back tears. "Thanks. Uh. Thank you."

He doesn't look at Finn as the silence thickens around them. Turning to face the window, he wipes his eyes on the back of his hands. Until now he hadn't realized how long he had been floundering alone.

"Alright," Finn sighs, reaching over to grip Étienne's shoulder. "I'm getting you a coffee."

"Oh no, God, you've done enough—"

"And donuts!" Finn declares, hammering a drumroll on the top of his steering wheel with his palms.

Étienne laughs, sniffing back his tears and picking an invisible speck of lint from his jeans. "Thanks."

"You're a Vixen now," Finn shrugs, as though it's the easiest thing in the world to say. "We've got your back."

It means more than he could ever know.

EIGHT

Étienne's touch haunts Jordan. It sears her skin all the way home. The scent of his body clings to her, snatching the air from her throat before she has time to breathe it in fully. By the time she pulls up outside her home, she still can't think of anything but him.

"It's just a crush," she tells herself for the fiftieth time since she left the factory. "Just a little crush. It'll pass."

The flashing light on the top of her cell phone makes her stomach drop. Three missed calls from Mia and a text which reads: *call me.*

It could be anything, just a note the lead singer forgot to give her before she bolted from the rehearsal room. It could also be questions about hers and Étienne's blatant and entirely unprofessional eye-fucking.

The sound of that camera shutter torments her. If she calls Finn and asks him to delete it, it's an admission of guilt. She'll have to tell him the specific photo she wants him to delete. How would she even describe it.

Whatever it was that passed between her and Étienne

they were caught at it. Half of her wants to see the picture, wants to analyze and overthink it. And half of her wants to hunt down Finn, steal his phone and throw it into an active volcano before anyone else can see.

But perhaps she's too late. It could have already been seen by the whole band. It could even be up on their website and social media by now. The thought of that chills her. She clears her throat and waits for Mia to answer.

"You okay?" The singer's voice comes abruptly after three rings.

"Yeah, I'm good." Jordan winces at the uncertainty in her voice. "You?"

The silence which follows only lasts a second or two, but to Jordan it's an eternity. When Mia speaks again her voice is lowered. "How did you feel about today?"

"About?"

"Finn," she whispers. "You haven't seen him since the day after the wedding."

"Oh…" Jordan chuckles, relieved. "Yeah, no that's totally over. Totally. He's just Finn."

"Good."

"I think it was just a combination of alcohol, wedding emotions and seeing him all… domesticated."

Mia laughs. "Yeah, I'm glad. We definitely don't need drama like that right now. We already have to deal with Étienne."

The sound of his name alone forces the air from Jordan's lungs. She runs her thumb across her fingertips of the hand which had rested on his shoulder. He'd felt strong, sturdy, and God, he'd smelled so good. "He sang great today."

"Yeah… I thought so too. He sounds great, but… I

mean, he ran out of rehearsals. What am I supposed to do if he gets stage fright at the festival?"

In the silence which follows Jordan's mind searches, grasping for an answer, but she comes up with nothing.

"Does he make you uncomfortable?" Mia asks quietly.

Jordan freezes. Flashes of hot and cold panic dart through her body. She has never been good at hiding her emotions, but her discomfort isn't because of him or anything he's done. It's because no matter how hard she tries, she can't stop thinking about him. "Oh, no it's okay. Nothing I can't handle."

"Are you sure? Because if you say the word his ass is out the door."

"I'm sure."

That's the last thing she wants. Singing with Vixen's Wail obviously means a lot to Étienne; if it didn't, he wouldn't have been so nervous. So, she'll just have to learn to hide her inability to be in the same room as him without making an ass of herself.

"Okay," Mia sighs. "This festival could be huge for us. He stays for now, but if you change your mind just say the word."

"I will, thanks."

"Later."

"Later." Jordan ends the call and leans back in the car seat.

It's ridiculous. All she had wanted was a simple one-night stand, but all she has to show for it is a tangled mess of emotions. And now she and Étienne have to work together. And she hasn't even gotten one measly orgasm out of it.

She lets out an exasperated moan and buries her face in her hands. "Fuck this."

At least the first rehearsal is over with. Hopefully soon he'll just blend into the furniture. If he doesn't, she's going to have even more problems on her hands.

The first sip of coffee on Étienne's tired throat is a balm. Rain taps on the roof of the van and speckles the windshield, a sound which always reminds him of long journeys with his parents. He sits back, warmed by the drink and the air blowing through the van's heaters as Finn takes a chocolate coated donut from a half-dozen box.

"Help yourself," the drummer tells him, setting the box on the dashboard.

"Thank you.

"Don't mention it."

They eat and sip in silence as the van thrums around them. This would never have happened with his old band. They were all business, meeting a couple of times a week in hotel parking lots, playing other people's songs at weddings and birthdays and then straight back home. Only ever communicating via email. Never with donuts.

"Okay," Finn says, stuffing the remaining quarter of his donut into his cheek and wiping his fingers on a napkin. "Is there anything you want to talk about?"

Where to begin? His money troubles, his newly founded performance anxiety, or the fact he's infatuated with one of his bandmates. "I just...I kind of feel like I'm sinking, and Vixen's Wail is this life raft, but if I climb in, I might take you all under with me."

"We're good swimmers," Finn shrugs. "And we take care of each other. I love every member of the band, you know, I'd do anything for them. And that includes you now."

But only for the next three weeks. After that he'll be on his way. Sure, if the songs he sings on are successful, he might get asked to perform at a gig or two, but he isn't fully a member of the band. He appreciates the big guy's kindness, but the sentiment rings a little hollow. Taking a sip of his coffee, he takes a donut from the dash and places it on a napkin on his thigh.

"What do you think of the band?" Finn asks, staring straight ahead as he raises the cup to his lips. "Is it working out how you thought it would?"

"You're all great," Étienne says truthfully. "It's truly an honor to play with you all."

"The pleasure's ours." The drummer smiles and takes another donut from the box. He glances over as Étienne raises the cup to his lips and says flatly, "Although probably mostly Jordan's."

Étienne chokes on his coffee, coughing into his elbow as Finn beats his back. By the time he's collected himself his throat is rawer than ever, and the blush on his cheeks has risen far above the safe shelter of his beard.

Finn laughs quietly as he resumes eating. "Sorry."

Shooting him a disgruntled glare, Étienne clears his throat one last time. "She's nice."

"Sure. And that's all, is it?"

"That's all," Étienne asserts. There's no way he's going to admit those feelings, even if Finn keeps throwing sly, knowing looks his way.

"I'm just saying," Finn sighs. "The air pretty much crackles around the two of you."

Nerves flutter in Étienne's chest. He'd be lying if he said

he didn't feel it too. And he'd be lying if having someone else notice their chemistry isn't a wonderful feeling. "She seems pretty cool."

The drummer grins and sits back, victorious. "Yeah, I figured. Just be careful. Dating band members can be complicated." He shrugs as Étienne raises an inquisitive eyebrow. "Way, *way* back Mia and I dated for a little while, and the break-up was pretty much as good as you can expect a break-up to be. I mean, obviously, we still work together, we're best friends, and we're both very happily married. But the fans… shit, some of them will not let that ship sail. It was hard to move on while being constantly reminded of the good times. Even now we get the occasional message begging us to get back together."

Étienne stares at the rain-specked windshield and runs his fingers around the rim of his coffee cup. "That's rough."

Finn shrugs and takes the lid from his coffee cup. "We can laugh about it now, but at the time it was hard. And that was a mutual, basically drama-free break-up. There have been other break-ups in the band, and those were…Jesus… they were bad."

"But who's to say we'd even break up?" The question leaves him before he can stop it. "You're making it sound like we're doomed."

"No. God, no I don't mean that at all. It's just a cautionary tale of the perils of loving a Vixen. But believe me, I also know what it's like to meet someone and to just feel that…that…"

"Detonation."

"Right," Finn smiles and sips his coffee. "Yeah. It's not just a spark. It's feeling everything that you thought you knew detonate, and then the pieces fall exactly where they should."

Étienne watches the steam rise and coil from the hole in the lid of his cup. Right now, the parts of him are still up in the air, tumbling and falling. He doesn't know where they'll land or whether he'll even know himself when they do. All he knows is that from the moment Jordan sat beside him at the bar, his world changed in some immeasurable way.

"I barely even know her." Étienne shrugs and tries to keep up the appearance of disinterest, but he suspects he's failing. The heat on his cheeks is so intense he knows he must be blushing. He has never been good at hiding it.

"Well, Baby Bear, you've got about three weeks of rehearsals and performing together. Time to get to know each other better."

"I don't know, man—"

"Maybe it'll come to nothing, but in ten years of knowing Jordan, I've never seen her look at someone the way she looks at you."

Étienne's heart lifts. Three weeks. It feels like forever, but he knows it will go by in a blur. But even if he does get to know her, the fact still remains that she might not be interested in him. She had made it clear on the day of his audition that they were purely professional.

Then again, that problem will solve itself after Ghoulfest.

He can't deny their chemistry, but even if it is mutual and she's as drawn to him as he is to her, that attraction could be purely physical. As much as he wants her, as much as he *craves* her, his heart needs her even more than his body does.

Finn clears his throat. "By the way, speaking of fans, I'll be posting the photo of us all together over the weekend and announcing your duets with Mia, so… you know… prepare your inbox."

He is not prepared.

The second Étienne wakes up that Saturday morning, his stomach lurches. Warm light filters through the gap in his curtains, shining on his phone screen as it vibrates on his bedside table. The persistent hum of constant notifications confirms his fear.

Vixen's Wail's fans know about him.

Rubbing the sleep from his eyes he rolls onto his back and grabs the phone. It takes him a little while to wade through the notifications and friend requests and find the original post, but when he does, his heart stops. There's a group photo. It's *the* group photo. He hones-in on the image of him and Jordan, arms wrapped around each other, their eyes locked. It's unmistakable, it's intimate, and god, do they ever look good together.

Wearing nothing but his boxers, he feels even more exposed, and even more like he's doing something he shouldn't. He covers his body with his bedsheets and peers more closely at the image.

Her breasts are pressed against him, her arm draped over his shoulder, her fingers lightly brushing the top of his bicep. That hadn't even registered in his mind at the time. There has to be less than an inch between the tips of their noses. It would have taken so little for him to kiss her.

Rubbing his hand over his face he tries to push away the thought that he blew his only chance.

The caption above the image catches his eye.

Bonjour Wailers! We are beyond fucking excited to announce our collaboration

with the très magnifique Étienne Moore, who will be duetting with Mia on two

tracks ON OUR UPCOMING BRAND FUCKING NEW ALBUM HOLY SHIT!

It's absolutely undoubtedly written by Finn and it seems to have gone over well with the fans. The post has hundreds of likes already, and just as many comments.

Oh damn, Finn isn't the token hot guy of the band anymore.
I've only known of Étienne for thirty seconds, and already I would fight every
one of you for him.
Oof Étienne. Oui oui. Le sploosh.

He scrolls, his ego suitably stroked. Of course, there are hobbit comments because there always are, but they barely register any more. The fans seem to approve of him, or at least, of his looks.

One comment gives him pause.

Um… are you all seeing the fucking TENSION between him and Jordan? Damn
girl, get some.

The replies to that are too tempting to ignore. He clicks to show the whole thread and all at once his biggest fears and wildest fantasies are confirmed.

Wait, are they dating?
They're definitely fucking.
Holy shit you're right. Jordo stole my man.
I think you mean this random French dude stole my Jordo!

There are a lot of emojis; eggplants, water droplets,

tongues, smirking faces, crying faces. Finn wasn't kidding, the fans are intense.

It's all a little too much.

He closes the tab on his phone and looks over his texts instead. There's one from Finn which reads: *You're famous!!!*

There's another from his old band's guitarist, Dan, simply stating: *fuck you.*

Some irrational part of him is a little saddened that there's nothing there from Jordan. No comments or texts so he can judge her reaction. He scrolls back up to the photo, remembering the sensation of her arm draped around his shoulders, and her breasts, soft and warm against his upper arm. He'd moved that arm instinctively and she'd only moved in closer, pressing her chest to his. Putting his arm on her waist might have crossed the line, but in the moment, it seemed she was just as into him as he was into her.

He lets his empty hand drift down, over the soft, hairy slope of his stomach until he slips his hand inside his boxers. His cock is hard as it is most mornings. It's built like the rest of him, a little on the shorter side, but thick, and far too easily smitten. His breath catches as he begins to stroke himself.

His hand had fit so perfectly on her waist, her soft sumptuous curves beneath his fingers, her eyes blazing into his; that warm, hypnotic hazel. He sets a gentle pace as he puts the phone down and closes his eyes. There he can imagine them alone together, her warm body fully pressed to him as she takes his hand in hers and ties it to the bed frame.

That's what he wants. To be tethered to the bed. To be hers.

He moans softly, picturing her naked on top of him, rolling her hips in time with his strokes. She arches her back a little as she teases his body, caressing his stomach, working her way up to his chest, her fingers teasing his nipples as he's helpless beneath her. He imagines her tits, soft and heavy, swaying back and forth with her movements, her nipples pink like her hair. Like her lips.

His toes curl as he envisages her using his body to pleasure herself, back arched while she comes, and all he can do is watch her ride him. He's close, so close, his orgasm building and coiling ready to tear through him.

He pulls the covers back and bucks his hips, thrusting up into his fist, desperate for release, and when he comes, he presses his head back into the pillow, gasping and moaning her name.

In the moments which follow, he listens to his slowing breath, and the near constant buzz of his phone. It seems everyone knows how he feels about her. Everyone but her.

NINE

That asshole Finn isn't answering his phone.

Logically Jordan knows it's because he's probably busy, but she can't shake the feeling he's sitting there cackling away watching it ring out and knowing exactly why she's calling. Beth must have taken ten photos that day. Why the fuck did it have to be that one?

"Hey this is Finn, leave a message baybeee."

She sighs and ends the call. Her laptop glows on the arm of her couch, the soft whir of its fan like distant laughter. Her heart beats hard, pumping scalding blood through her trembling body.

She doesn't have her own social media accounts—not since Danny—but every once in a while, she'll check the band's forums.

The lack of social media makes everything simpler. No fans tempted to overstep boundaries into her personal life, no chance of her asshole ex hunting her down. The fans don't even know her surname. It's more than just a mysterious persona. It's armor.

She slumps back down on the couch and scrolls through the comments on the picture. At least she's not alone in thinking Étienne is hot. And jeez, the picture of them together…they're clinched, intense, and downright beautiful together. The fans see it, it's impossible not to, and already there are rumors that Étienne and Jordan are dating.

Um… are you all seeing the fucking TENSION between him and Jordan? Damn girl, get some.

She leans against the arm of the couch, bracing herself with her elbow as she presses the knuckles of her fingers to her lips. Fucking Finn.

She no longer has the urge to throw his phone into an active volcano. No. Now she wants to throw him into one.

The replies to the "get some" comment are definitely something. Speculation, jealousy, and a few people making leaps that would win gold in the Conclusion Olympics. Not only are they apparently dating but have been for years. Jeez.

Her fingers twitch with the urge to put them straight, but she knows from experience those kinds of rumors are best to ignore and let them die down.

She quickly minimizes that thread and scrolls up again. A new top comment is racking up the likes and replies, one from a user named VIXENETI.

Thanks for the warm welcome, Wailers. I can't wait to show you what we're working on. I think you're going to love it. Also, I'm not actually French. XO

She smiles, grateful he hasn't addressed the rumors. It's a gracious response, humble in the face of all that praise and comment after comment about his sexiness. But maybe, just maybe it isn't humble. Maybe he's embarrassed, over-whelmed, maybe he's just as mortified by it all as she is.

Before she can talk her way out of it, she creates an account on the forum, choosing VIXENJORDO as her user-name. Holding her breath, she sends him a buddy request and types out a welcome message.

VIXENJORDO: Hey, I hope you're doing okay. Our fans are great, but I know it can be a lot. If you need to chat let me know. Jordan.

She hits send and sits back, trying to fend off the voice telling her she's making a huge mistake. The message isn't flirty, not in the slightest, but maybe he'll misconstrue it, or maybe things will turn that way. The evidence she can't trust herself around him is right in front of her face, with over a thousand likes and counting.

No, it's absurd. She needs to find a way to fix it. But as she searches for a delete message button, his reply pops up.

VIXENETI: *Hi. Yeah, it's pretty nuts. Thank you for reaching out. It means a lot. I'll be okay, I'm a big boy*

VIXENETI: *(figuratively speaking, obviously)*

She reads the messages over and over. Is he… *flirting?*

Biting down a nervous smile, she tries to tell herself her heart is just racing because she's happy he's okay. Really, *really* happy. A hundred variations of big boy comments roll through her mind. She's not going there.

No.

Absolutely not.

VIXENJORDO: *Glad to hear it.*

VIXENJORDO: *Finn could've chosen a photo of us both looking at the camera though.*

As soon as she sends it, she knows that acknowledging the eye-fucking elephant in the room is a risk, one she didn't calculate, and one she can't take back.

VIXENETI: *yeah...*
VIXENETI: *Hey, at least we're pretty.*

A surge of giddiness rolls through her body as she fights back a grin. Her breath is shallow and her cheeks burning.

VIXENJORDO: *Very true.*

She sits back, smiling as three dots ripple across the message box showing he's typing something. The ripples become sporadic, stopping and starting, and the more time that passes, the more she's certain she needs to get the hell off that website.

While she waits, she goes back to the photo and zooms in on the pair of them. The look in his eyes is magnetic. She tries to imagine she's an outsider looking in, ignoring the heat she had felt in that moment.

But even then, she sees it. It's hunger, need, desire. And reverence.

Her chest tightens. She tries to deny it to herself but it's impossible. He looks at her as though there *is* only her, and she's looking at him the same way. The rest of the band smile at the camera, completely unaware of what is going on just a few feet away from them. She hadn't even really noticed them, and that scares her. Because in that moment, the

Vixens, who she loves more than anyone, were entirely forgotten.

She returns to the messages and finds his dots have stopped entirely. She knows she should leave it, but the pull is impossible to resist.

VIXENJORDO: *See you at practice.*

He doesn't reply. Definitely for the best.

She closes the window entirely and is about to log out of the forum when a comment beneath the photo sends a bolt of icy fear through her heart. It isn't so much the comment though, which is just a laughing crying emoji. It's the username, one she had blocked on all her social media accounts before deleting them for good.

That username is DannyShreds.

É tienne hears Finn's van approach long before he sees it. Blasting demonic music grows louder and louder, announcing the drummer's arrival. As the beat-up black van pulls around the corner into his street, Étienne cringes as his neighbors' blinds twitch.

His phone vibrates in his hand as yet another text from his old bandmate flashes across the screen:

I hope you're fucking happy.

He sighs and deletes the message. There's only so long his old guitarist can stay jealous and angry for before he'll just give up. It has been a few days since the picture of Étienne and the band was posted on their social media, and since then he's received a fair few shitty messages from his hot-headed former bandmate. The texts don't get to him though. They worked together for six years, and in that time, he built a thick skin to block out the asshole's insults.

The sigh of Finn's van's brakes pushes them from his mind altogether.

"Gooooood morning, Baby Bear!" Finn yells over the music as Étienne climbs up into the passenger seat.

"Morning," Étienne chuckles as he fastens his seatbelt. It is a good morning. He'll spend the day singing, and he'll get to see Jordan.

He hasn't spoken to her since that day on the forum. Since he had come so close to asking her out.

VIXENETI: *I was wondering if you would like to come for a drink with me?*

The message had taken him almost five nerve-wracking minutes to type and only seconds to delete. He had slammed his laptop shut and refused to even look at it for the rest of the weekend.

"Hey, so…one sec," Finn pauses as he turns down the volume on the stereo. "We're booked in to record the singles next Friday."

Étienne's stomach flips. "So soon."

"Well, that'll leave us just under two weeks until the festival. We're having to crunch but it'll be worth it… hopefully."

The thought closes Étienne's airways. He's only played with the band once, and already time is getting away from him. "Shit."

"I know. Crunch time, baby."

By the time they pull up to the factory Étienne is nervous

again; uncertain of his future, and uncertain of his feelings. He hops down from the van, casting a guilty glance at his own useless vehicle still waiting in the parking lot, before he follows Finn inside. Now that they're out of the van Étienne can see the design on the drummer's black t-shirt. The Vixen's Wail logo is emblazoned in red across his chest. Beneath that is a sexy pinup devil girl and "I heart Finn" scrawled across his round stomach.

"Nice shirt."

"Thanks. I can order you one if you like? Oh, and by the way," Finn grins as they head up the stairs. "I hope the announcement wasn't too much."

It takes Étienne a moment to realize he means the photo and the fans on the forum. "The fans were fine."

"Good."

"But why that picture?"

The only reply comes from the tinkling keys in the lock as the big guy unlocks the rehearsal room. They enter and for once it's silent and empty, though not for long. Finn flips on the lights and heads toward an acoustic guitar which was waiting for them on a stand, and sits down to pluck a tune, as if he can't bear to be away from music for any stretch of time. Either that or he doesn't want to answer.

"She saw it," Étienne says as he sets his jacket down and begins to set up his mic stand. "She messaged me after you posted it."

Finn stops plucking. "Wait, Jordan *messaged* you?"

"Yeah? Just a couple of times and nothing flirty or anything."

"*The* Jordan? Cello player, purple hair…"

"Pink hair," Étienne corrects. "It's pink now. And yeah. At least it said it was her."

He chuckles. "Well, Jordan doesn't message anyone. She never even goes on the forums, doesn't use any kind of social media. If it was her, then I'd say she's making some pretty fucking big exceptions for you."

Étienne can't help but smile. Of course there's every chance the big guy could be completely wrong, but if he isn't… His heart skips. "Finn, I like her. I really do."

The drummer chuckles. "No shit."

"I just don't know what to say to her. One minute she seems like she's into me too, and the next she can't stand to be around me."

"Jordan is…" The drummer raises his eyes to the ceiling as his chest inflates. "She has definitely been hurt before. It's not my place to tell you what went down, but I think she's hesitant to let people in."

Étienne nods. He gets it, but he almost envies her that ability. Letting people in has never been difficult for him, and often that's the problem. He falls for people too hard and too fast, mistaking casual hookups for the start of something more.

"Whatever you do," Finn sighs as he begins plucking the guitar once more. "Don't write a song about her."

Étienne chuckles and scratches his aching chest. "I couldn't even if I tried. But when I sing, every damn note is for her. When I froze up, I pictured the two of us together and imagined I was just singing to her. It helped. I don't know… it's… I know it sounds so corny."

"No, I get it," Finn says quietly. "I do."

Finn's van is already outside the factory, parked beside Étienne's car when Jordan arrives. She hurries upstairs to their rehearsal room, her anxiety like a swarm crawling across her skin, as it has been all weekend. The thought of Danny lurking on their forums has churned her stomach ever since she saw his username. She needs a moderator to block him, which means she needs Finn. But before she gets to the rehearsal room door, she pauses.

Soft, melodic, acoustic music accompanies the most beautiful, passionate male voice she has ever heard. Right away she knows it's Étienne. That voice could lure ships to rocks.

Her skin prickles at the sound and her breath catches as he reaches a crescendo, his rich, powerful sound striking through her heart and straight into her soul. Even if she never saw how devastatingly, unfairly handsome he is, she would fall for his voice alone.

Forcing out a breath, she reminds herself he is just a friend and a coworker. Nothing more. Absolutely nothing. Her knees are just turning to jelly because of the climb up the stairs.

She lets his song end and the tingles on the surface of her skin finish their dance before opening the door.

Étienne stands as she enters, stepping away from Finn and back to his mic stand. There's a tension in the room which tells her she caught them doing something they didn't want to be discovered.

And inconsiderately, Étienne looks even better today. The neckline of his t-shirt is a little lower, showing a hint of dark chest hair. His jeans fit just tight enough over his round ass and thighs, tight enough to squeeze the air from her lungs.

Seeing him brings back the memory of being pressed against him. Not that she hasn't thought of it constantly since it happened. What she wouldn't give to be that close to him again.

Curling her fingers at her side, she smiles in greeting. "Good morning."

"Morning," Étienne replies curtly, raising his arm to wipe his forehead on the back of his hand.

She desperately tries not to look at the definition in his arms. But she fails. God she spectacularly fails. "Hey, um, Finn, can I talk to you a sec?"

Thankfully, the larger man nods and stands, setting his acoustic guitar on a stand beside him. "Sure."

She holds the door open for him, and together they step out into the privacy of the corridor.

"What's up?" he asks, shoving his hands into the pockets of his jeans. "If this is about the photo—"

"No." She pulls in a breath. "I was on the Vixen forum over the weekend and I think…" She lowers her voice further, as though speaking his name will somehow summon him. "I think one of the people on there was Danny."

Finn's eyes grow wide. "Oh shit." He breathes long and slow through his nose, nostrils flaring like a bull about to charge. "Do you remember the username?"

"DannyShreds." She folds her arms over her chest. "It's the username he always used way back when everything happened."

"Did he say anything to you?"

"No. No he just commented on the picture with Étienne. It wasn't offensive or anything like that, I just… I saw the name and my heart stopped." She leans back against the wall beside Finn. "I guess it might not actually be him, just someone with the same username. I don't know. Danny isn't exactly an unusual name."

"Alright. I'll keep a close eye on the user and if he even considers putting a toe out of line, he's out of there. And if you have any trouble, any at all, just let me know."

Jordan smiles up at him. Every one of the Vixens had stood by her side throughout that mess, and they still do, but Finn was the one who took it upon himself to be her protector when Danny was at his worst. Finn would always walk her to her car to make sure she was safe, he helped her scrub the profanities off the brickwork of her house. The one time Danny had barged into rehearsal demanding answers was the only time Finn had ever been intimidating, and god, she was thankful for it. She has always felt safe knowing she can count on him for anything.

He reaches over and pulls her into a side hug. "Shit. I'm so sorry I ignored your calls. I figured you were pissed about the photo."

Jordan scowls indignantly at him. "You fucker."

"Yeah. Oh, hey while we're out here, Étienne's car died last time we were here. I have a guy coming to pick it up today. I took him home but I'm kind of rushed tonight. Could you take him? He lives on your side of town."

Her heart kicks up its rhythm. "Uh…"

"Please? I promised Beth we'd do something special tonight. He lives really close to you anyway." He bends his knees a little and puts his hands together as though he's praying to her. But it's the damned puppy eyes which win her over.

"I— ugh yes."

Bastard.

TEN

É tienne is exhausted by the end of practice, his throat shredded, his body aching, but his heart is full. He hasn't frozen once since that first day. His stage fright appears to have been cured. Sure, he's a little nervous singing in front of the whole band, but when he sings to Jordan, when he imagines they are the only two people in the room, he can breathe again.

His phone vibrates against his thigh. Even without looking, nausea rises in his stomach, and when he pulls the phone out his suspicions are confirmed.

Stop ignoring me, dude. We need to talk.

As with the other texts he's received from his old bandmate, he deletes it and tries to forget. He has to remind himself that he has done nothing wrong. Dan was the one who said they should split and that their band, Eclectic Boogaloo was going nowhere. It's hardly Étienne's fault that he has found another band while Dan apparently hasn't.

"Hey, Étienne, you ready?"

He stiffens a little at the sound of Jordan's voice before turning to face her. Despite the fact they've spent the day together, he still gets flustered at the sight of her. "For?"

"To go home," she says as she pulls her thick grey hoodie over her shoulders.

Confused, he glances at Finn. The drummer sits grinning behind his kit, before raising his big shoulders in an innocent shrug. "I have a few things to take care of here. Jordo will look after you though. Just make sure you kids buckle up. And, you know, make safe choices."

When Étienne turns back around to face Jordan, he catches her giving Finn some serious stink-eye. Cautiously he asks her, "Are you sure?"

"Yeah," she sighs, sounding anything less than sure. "You're over on my side of town anyway, apparently."

They say goodbye to the rest of the band and make their way out into the hallway. Their footsteps set a fast and heavy beat as they pick up their pace, both clearly desperate to get this awkwardness over with, though Étienne suspects for very different reasons.

The silence between them lasts until they get outside and into the clear night. Jordan stops, bathed in the white security light outside the front of the door and clears her throat. "You were amazing today. Again. You always are."

Étienne's ears begin to burn immediately but it's not like he isn't used to praise. Back when his old band played weddings, he was constantly complimented, and occasionally hit on because of his voice, but it's different coming from her. "Thanks. You were too. As always."

She smiles and tucks a loose strand of hair behind her ear, shivering as she pulls her keys out of her purse. It's a brisk fall evening, reminding them that October is well under way. Halloween night draws ever closer, and with it, Ghoulfest. He tries not to think about it too much. As they make their way across the parking lot through the fading dusk light, he imagines a world where he can hold her hand, or put his arm around her to help keep her warm.

"Do you want my jacket?" The question leaves him unexpectedly, and judging by the way she looks at him, it's just as bizarre to her.

"No, I'm alright. I don't think it would fit me anyway. But thank you."

They climb into her car and she waits for him to put his address into her GPS. When they set off, the silence between them is heavier than any he's known. Confined with her like this, he's all too aware of himself, of the awkward position of his hands on his lap, the heat emanating from his palms as they press against his thighs. The longer the silence extends the longer he has to think, to feel. He has to do something. He has to say *something*.

"How did you start playing cello?" He asks, his voice rough.

She doesn't take her eyes from the road. "Probably the same way you started singing. I started in school and just kept on going."

He nods, swallowing the lump in his throat. "It's beautiful."

"Thank you."

God, he can't bear it. He has never wanted anyone more in his life and this awkwardness between them is torture.

"Hey," she says, glancing toward him for a second. "I need to stop for gas. Is that okay?"

"Sure."

Her blinkers click, counting every agonizing moment and his mouth dries out as they turn and her hands glide along the steering wheel. He can't go on like this. He has to find some way to cope with the permanent ache, the longing he feels for her with every cell of his body. Because he does want her, desperately, but she stipulated when he took the job that this would remain purely professional. He's spectacularly failing at that.

She pulls onto the forecourt and stops beside a gas pump. "I'll just be a second," she mutters.

He turns to look at her, his face burning as unasked questions and undisclosed desire rage through his mind. It's only been days, and they still have weeks of this. He can't. He has to get it into the open. He has to. And whatever her answer is, even if she flat-out rejects him, he'll accept. But whatever she says it has to be better than not knowing.

He swallows his pride and pulls in a breath. "Jordan?"

At the sound of her name on Étienne's lips, she's lost. Jordan turns back to face him. Light glimmers in his eyes, his face so yearning and desperate, and in that moment she's no longer in control.

Her lips graze his and at their first touch a moan escapes him which reverberates through her entire body. Right away she wants more, her body craving his warmth and the release she has craved since the moment she laid eyes on him.

But he doesn't kiss her back.

His lips are soft and still beneath hers. Mortified, she pulls away, afraid she's made a mistake, raising her fingers to her lips in horror at what she's done. "I'm so sor—"

Her apology is lost to her shuttering breath as he gently takes her hand away from her mouth. His other hand goes to the back of her head, pulling her to him. His eyes are half-lidded and this time his lips are ready. He kisses like she knew he would, slow and confident, like he knows she's more than happy for this to go on all night.

Every movement of his lips sends bursts of pleasure and need coursing through her body. She leans into him until the car's lever jabs her in her right thigh, craving more, demanding more, her fingers gripping the neckline of his shirt, her knuckles rasping against the coarse patch of his dark chest hair.

The shrill blare of a car's horn behind them pulls them apart.

"Shit," she hisses as she grabs her purse from the back seat, casting a glance over her shoulder at the line of cars and trucks waiting for the gas pump behind them.

She can't look at Étienne as she climbs out of her car, closes the door behind her and pulls out her debit card with shaking fingers. The cold wind whips around her, soothing her scorching skin as she waves an apology and flashes an insincere smile at the cars behind.

Gulping down air, she swipes her card and begins to pump the gas, but every breath comes at a price. Her chest and stomach ache with every lungful, a petulant urge coursing through her body, demanding she get back in the car and take more from him. But she can't. He's her band-mate. It should never have happened, and it can't happen again. No matter how much she wants him.

Breathless, Étienne sits alone in the dark, his mind racing to make sense of what just happened. His heart pounds in his ears, a drum driving him to action, pumping liquid fire to all the parts of him which crave her.

A moment later her door opens, and she slumps back into the driver's seat, tossing her purse into the back. "I'm done."

They set off, pulling out of the gas station and back on to the road, the GPS guiding them to his apartment. It isn't much further, but in the cloying silence it may as well be the other side of the universe.

"Are you okay?" she asks as they wait at a stop light.

He sighs. "Yeah. I'm good."

He isn't.

He can't think of anything beyond how good she felt, how right, and how lost he is without her. His lips are tingling, his cock is hot and hard, straining against the faded black denim of his jeans as he curls his fingers into his palms. "Are you?"

She drags in a deep breath and lets her shoulders slouch. "I think we need to talk about…well… I guess everything."

"Talking's good."

She chuckles a little. "Yeah."

"I like you, Jordan." He blurts it out. "God, I really fucking do."

She stares straight ahead, focusing on the road. Red and white lights strobe across her face, illuminating the lips he's so drunk on. From the heavy rise and fall of her chest he suspects she's having as hard a time breathing as he is.

"I like you too," she says at last.

Relief makes his heart soar as she reaches over with her

right hand and puts it on his. Her palms are soft and warm against the back of his hand.

She glances over at him. "But we can't do this."

His heart sinks. "But you kissed me."

"I know." She withdraws her hand, wedging it between her thighs. "I shouldn't have, but I just... I don't know. I can't."

He's heard it before, so many times. Nice to look at, good for a fuck, but not the type of guy you'd want to be seen in public with. Hell, he's been dumped before because his date was worried that she couldn't comfortably wear high heels without it feeling like she was walking beside a child. Add to that his current financial situation and he knows he's hardly a man she'd be proud to introduce to her family.

He's used to it, but it doesn't mean it hurts any less, and it doesn't mean he believes it either. He deserves better.

He's tired of being disposable.

She pulls up to his apartment and turns away from him to look out of her window. "I'm so sorry, Étienne."

"May I ask why?" Étienne's voice is quiet and level, but the shallow rise and fall of his chest indicates that inside he's anything but. "I mean, if it was just that you're not into me then I wouldn't ask, but you came on to me at the wedding, you kissed me back there, but now you don't want me?"

Jordan is glad of the darkness in the car which hides the redness on her face. He's right. He deserves an explanation. But no matter how she phrases it in her head, she can't get the words to come.

"What did I do wrong?" he asks.

"Nothing. Nothing at all."

Étienne sighs softly. "Okay. I think I know why. It has happened before, and it always boils down to the way I look." He chuckles bitterly and shakes his head. "I'm not going to fake modesty about this. I know I'm good looking, but I also know I'm five foot five and I don't have abs or—"

"No," Jordan blurts. "It isn't that. Not at all."

On the contrary, she loves how he looks. He's the perfect height to kiss so neither of them have to stretch or stoop. The shape of his body is irresistible to her, so irresistible she's thought of nothing else since she first laid eyes on him.

"Then, what?" He turns to face her, constellations of overhead street lights shining in his eyes. "Because I feel something when I'm with you, Jordan, and maybe I'm way off but I think you feel it too."

She lowers her head and forces a breath in. "I do."

"Then what are you afraid of?"

A dam breaks inside her and a torrent of words pours from her. "That if I give in and let myself fall for you the way that I want to, it'll tear the band apart. It's happened to me before. I've been here, Étienne. I know how this plays out. It's too complicated to date another band member, and it isn't fair to the other Vixens."

"What isn't?"

"The fallout when we break up."

"Why do you think we'd break up?"

Jordan's heart thrums as Étienne turns his body sideways in his seat and takes her hand in his. His thumb skims the peaks of her knuckles, gentle caresses which send pulses of electricity shooting through her veins. Her lips still tingle from the rasp of his beard. It's every bit as cruel as it is delicious.

She stares at the shadowed footwell beneath her, focusing on the darkness because if she looks at Étienne, she doesn't know if she can stop from kissing him again.

"Look…" His voice is shaking slightly. "I have less than three weeks until my time with Vixen's Wail is up anyway. If by the festival you never want to see me again, then I'll walk away after we perform, and the band carries on as normal. I'd never do anything to hurt you or the band."

Her breath catches in her throat, snagged on a tiny shred of hope. She raises her eyes to meet his, and the sight of him winds her. Damn those gentle eyes and pouty lips. A desperate need for him burns through her, a flash of wildfire cauterizing the wounds that have lain open on her heart for so long.

"Like a trial run?" she manages to say. Her throat is dry, her pulse beating hard and fast.

"Yeah." The corners of Étienne's mouth quirk up into a smile. "If that's what you need. We would only take it as far as we're both comfortable with. Maybe we could start small, go out for a coffee or… I don't know."

Her heart squeezes. No one has ever put that much consideration into her feelings before. "Do you have coffee in your apartment?"

His smile broadens. "Yeah, I do."

"Then let's start now."

Eleven

É tienne's fingers shake as he unlocks the door to his apartment and steps aside to let her in. Better to get this over with now, let her see that he doesn't have much to offer her financially. Still, his stomach tightens, anticipating rejection, or worse, ridicule.

She steps inside, into the center of his living room, her eyes rising to the popcorn textured ceiling, down to the photographs of his family which cover the walls. Having her in his space after over a week of wishing she were there is almost dreamlike.

What was he thinking? In desperation he had begged her to give them a chance. He couldn't bear to come so close to having her, only to be sent away. But now he has to deal with what that means. In three weeks, they could go their separate ways, never to see each other again. Who knows how smitten he'll be by then?

The corners of her eyes crease as she approaches the black and white image of his grandparents. They're locked in an embrace at the end of a pier, gazing deep into each other's eyes.

He breathes a little easier as he walks over to her side. "That's my grandaddy and mémé."

"Mémé?" She smiles at him. "And you said you didn't speak French."

He knows he has that dorky-ass smile on his face, the one where his nose crinkles, but he can't fight it off. She doesn't seem to care that his apartment is small or that all of his furniture is hand-me-downs.

Turning back to the photo she stares intently. "She's beautiful." She turns back to face him immediately, her gaze drifting across his features. "You have her eyes."

His breaths become shallow as Jordan's eyes lock to his, the hazel of her irises almost entirely overtaken by her pupils. Her lips part slightly and it takes all his willpower not to reach out for her, to take her by the waist and bring her into his arms. Every atom in his body pulls him toward her, longing for her, desperate to feel all of her. But if he does that, if he gives in to the need, he knows he might not be able to come back. She'd have him, his body, his heart, and soul and he would never be able to reclaim himself then.

"Can I get you anything?" His question makes her smile again. "Coffee? I think I have some hot chocolate."

Her eyes widen in excitement. "I'm never going to say no to hot chocolate."

"Right." He gestures to the couch, offering her a seat. "I'll be right back. Make yourself comfortable."

He hurries to the kitchen and turns on the electric stove. Taking a jug from the fridge he fills a saucepan with milk and presses the cold, empty container to his burning brow.

Condensation from the plastic, pools on his skin, running in tiny cold rivers down his forehead.

"What am I doing?" he whispers.

He knows he shouldn't, but damn, all he wants to do is kiss every inch of her. He wants to taste her, to have her on top of him, riding him until he forgets his own name and can only whimper hers.

Closing his eyes, he tries to shake the image of her, naked, straddling his hips as he lays back, tied down, but the harder he tries, the more vivid the image.

"Hey?"

Her voice almost causes him to drop the milk carton. Eyes wide open, he tries to regain his composure as she leans against the doorframe to his kitchen. She has taken off her hoodie, revealing the flowing, burgundy, sleeveless shirt she has on beneath. Her arms are soft and thick, the skin of their undersides a shade paler and dimpled. He could happily spend his whole life wrapped in those arms, searching out new shades in her hazel eyes.

"You okay?" he asks, hoping his arousal isn't too noticeable.

"I couldn't get comfortable."

"Oh." He sets down the carton. "Yeah, sorry it's a pretty crummy couch, I usually sit on the floor—"

She laughs quietly. "No. I mean, I couldn't stop thinking about something." Her top teeth graze the pillow of her lower lip in a way which sends a thrill of energy directly to his cock. "I know we said we'd take it slow, but… would it be okay if we try again?"

"Try what?"

She steps toward him, her eyes fixed on his lips as she closes the gap between them. "What we started in the car."

He nods. Her warm, soft stomach presses against his, her breasts brush against his chest. Gently, she nudges him backwards, until the cold, solid surface of the refrigerator is against his back. There's no doubt in his mind that she can feel his erection against her thigh. His heart beats so hard she probably feels his pulse throbbing through the air between them. It's a struggle to swallow. "God, yes."

Instinctively, his hand drifts up to her waist, his fingers pulling gently against her back to keep her close to him. Her throat twitches as though she's about to say something, but she doesn't speak.

With slow, tender movements, she reaches up and rasps her fingers through the scruff on his jaw.

Her lips graze his, a gentle, teasing caress which sends a wave of pleasure and excitement through his body. His fingers curl against her waist, desperate for more of her, but she teases him, torturing him with slow, featherlight kisses.

Every touch of her lips is a punch to his heart, a wave of heat from his temples to the pit of his belly. He could press on, lean into her and kiss her deeply, but he lets her set the pace. He likes it that way, wants her in complete control. And what exquisite torture it is.

Her hands skim the curves of his torso, her fingertips exploring the soft mound of his stomach. His toes curl inside his shoes as she reaches his chest, her thumbs strumming against his nipples before she works her way down to his biceps, never once taking her mouth from his.

The moan which escapes her is almost a purr.

With a sigh she pulls back, her eyes dark with desire. For a moment she looks as though she's about to say something. A crease deepens between her eyebrows. But no sooner has it appeared than her lips are back on his, her kiss deepening as she teases open his mouth with hers.

Running her fingernails over the short, cropped hair above his ears, she sends a shiver through his body. She sucks his lower lip as a moan escapes him, and her hands drop lower, exploring every inch of his torso.

His knees almost buckle as her fingertips return to the taught peaks of his nipples, sending bolts of pleasure shooting through him.

God, he wants her. No matter how many times he repeats the warning to himself, telling him to take it slow or he'll lose his heart, he still wants her. His whole body responds to her touch, goosebumps pebbling across his skin, his nipples tight and aching desperate for more, and his cock twitching with every movement of her hands, and every touch of her tongue against his.

He trails his hands down her back over the ample curve of her ass, squeezing her cheeks through the soft denim of her jeans. His body is on fire, his pulse hammering—

"Wait. Stop." She darts back from him, eyes wide, and he's pretty sure his heart stops at her command.

It's too much.

The moment he grabs her ass, her whole body freezes up, and right then and there she's back with Danny. Almost a decade later, and he still haunts her.

She steps back away from Étienne, one hand grasping at her chest as though she can control her panic.

"I'm sorry," Étienne gasps, his eyes wide, still dark with

lust, searching hers. His breath shakes as he holds up his palms. "God, I'm so sorry."

As she fights to steady her breath, she tells herself he's so unlike Danny.

Danny was tall and lean, long black hair and beard. He was also possessive and volatile and didn't give a shit about her needs or boundaries.

Her heart hammers as she lowers her eyes. "No, you didn't do anything wrong. I just… I panicked."

Bringing her fingers up to her tingling lips, she tries to brush away the longing sensation there, the need clouding her thoughts. Her body simultaneously tells her to run, yet still laments the distance between them.

The pan on the stove bubbles and hisses behind her.

"It was too much, wasn't it?" Étienne asks, seemingly unbothered by the pan boiling over. His voice shakes as the blush on his cheeks darkens further still. "I took it too far. I'm so sorry."

"We both did, I think." She takes half a step back, her skin cooling in the open air. "Too far and too fast. It's never happened before."

Étienne nods, and inhales sharply before pushing back from the fridge and hurrying over to the stove to turn off the pan. With him behind her, Jordan closes her eyes and forces a breath, every bit as frustrated with herself as she is relieved. He'd felt so good. If she concentrates, she can still feel him pressed against her, his lips on hers.

"Do you want me to go?" She isn't sure he hears her at first.

Her voice is so quiet and strained around the thickness in her throat. As she turns to face him, she can barely stand the sadness and longing in his eyes, the way his throat bobs while his gaze burns into her. It takes all her self-control not to wrap her arms around him, to seek warmth and comfort from his sturdy frame. Averting her eyes, she tries to focus on the brown stain of burned milk on the stove.

"I don't want you to, but I understand if you do." He rings a tea towel between his fingers.

"I don't want to," she says.

"There's just enough milk left. I can still make you a hot chocolate. If you want one?" With a sigh he frowns at the stove. "No, that's stupid, you probably don't want it now."

He *so* isn't Danny. For all his swagger he's soft, gentle and sweet. Watching him fumble in the kitchen is endearing. And as her anxiety fades and her heart beat returns to normal, she realizes it's also kind of sexy. But then, everything he does is sexy.

She's done with letting Danny corrupt every moment of passion. Somehow, he still manages to stain every aspect of her life, but she won't let him ruin Étienne for her.

"Is there enough for us both to have one?" she asks.

He grimaces at the brown stain on his stovetop and the steaming, foamy milk in the pan. "Uh, no. But I don't mind."

"How about we go halfsies and just talk?"

He raises his eyes to look at her and smiles. "Deal."

Stepping back to let him maneuver around the tiny kitchen, Jordan can't help but watch him. If she had a million guesses she would never have imagined Étienne's apartment to look the way it does. She might have expected a stereotypical bachelor pad, minimalist décor, black leather couch, and a lingering spicy scent of cologne in the air.

The truth is far harder to pin down to a style. Everything he owns is worn, lived-in. Possibly handed down from family or bought from a thrift store. Where she expected bare, minimalist walls there are photos of the people he loves and admires in mis-matched frames.

The mugs he takes out of the cupboard aren't trendy and Scandinavian like she might have guessed. One is white with the words "World's Okayest Singer" scrawled across it, and the other is tall and dark green, with a red and black plaid stag and "Happy Holidays" printed beneath.

"I'm sorry," he says with a grimace as he spoons cocoa powder into the mugs. "I don't really have people over often."

"It's no problem. I'm more disturbed by the inaccuracy of that." She points to the "World's Okayest Singer" mug.

Étienne chuckles, as he trickles the milk into the mug, stirring all the while. "Ah, yeah a gift from my former guitarist."

"Jerk."

"Yup." He sets the pan down on a cool burner and reaches up into the cupboard, raising on his tiptoes to pull out a clear plastic bag. "Marshmallows?"

She can't fight back the smile pulling at her lips. "Fuck yes."

Handing her the bag, he steps back allowing her to put in her own. "I would do it for you, but I tend to go overboard. If I was alone, I'd just fill the whole mug with them and eat them with a spoon."

Jordan chuckles. "Why do you have to be alone?"

"Because I want to hide the fact that I'm a hot mess for a little while longer, so you think I have my life at least somewhat together."

She narrows her eyes in playful disapproval as she drops eight mini marshmallows into her half cup of hot chocolate. "You're not a mess."

"Hot though?"

"Oh, absolutely."

He frowns, taking the bag from her. "Weird. I definitely remember you saying I was a six."

"Well, we weren't alone then." She presses her lips together, suppressing a laugh as true to his word, he dumps a full handful of marshmallows into the cup and grabs a spoon from a drawer. "And Finn's unbearable when he knows he's right."

A quirk of Étienne's eyebrows lets her know he knows what she means. He's off the charts.

She watches him, fascinated as he stirs his cup, melting the marshmallows in the chocolate and mixing the concoction into a pale brown goop. It's horrific, but the smile he gives her almost melts her too. Her breath stills as he puts the spoon between his lips, and slowly pulls it out clean. With a contented sigh, he closes his eyes. "Am I still hot?"

"Weirdly, but yeah."

"I can live with that. Do you want to go and sit down?"

She nods as she sips her own drink and follows him to the living room. It's hard to believe that only moments ago they shared such passion. Now, it's easy, comfortable. He stops beside the couch and lets her sit first. Somehow, he has the ability to set her completely at ease, and with that comes a renewed sense of desire.

When he settles beside her, the heat of his thick thigh next to hers makes her stomach somersault. It feels natural to be with him like this, close, intimate, no pressure. But in the moments between each spoonful of his marshmallow and chocolate monstrosity, she can tell he's suppressing what he wants to say. Twice now she's kissed him, and twice she's pushed him away. He deserves to know why.

"Okay." She sits forward and places her mug on his coffee table. "I think I should just be straight with you. And I don't know if this is going to sound ridiculous because I haven't really spoken about it to anyone other than the Vixens. But I trust you, and I guess you are technically a Vixen too anyway."

He sets his mug down too and turns a little to face her. The flex of his throat tells her he's just as nervous as she is. "Okay."

"So…" She draws a deep breath and pushes it out slowly. "You might have noticed I find it hard to connect with people, romantically."

TWELVE

Étienne listens as she opens up to him. Her words are a trickling stream, gradually eroding the defenses she's built up over the years. He's known his share of asshole bandmates, and though the man she describes remains anonymous, he is eerily similar to his own ex-guitarist.

But even though Dan was a moody asshole and thrived on putting him down, Étienne was never scared of him. He can only imagine the feeling of being afraid in his own home, of having to rely on someone like Finn to defend him because he feels helpless.

Jordan's eyes turn glassy as she confides in him, and it takes all his restraint not to open his arms and offer her solace. But he doesn't want to silence her.

"I haven't seen him in… God… eight years," she finishes, raising her eyes to the ceiling to fight back her tears. "But I still feel like he's lurking somewhere all the time, tainting everything in my life. And he almost ended Vixen's Wail altogether." She chuckles, glancing at Étienne's hand, which rests hot and heavy on his thigh. She reaches out and laces her fingers with him as though it's the most natural thing in the world to do. "I swore I'd never date another musician, especially not a Vixen."

He nods. As much as he wants her, he isn't going to insist she give anything more than she wants to. "That's understandable."

"But you kind of make things complicated." She leans forward, dipping her head so she can look him in the eye. "Because no matter how many times I tell myself it's a bad idea, I can't seem to stop wanting you. The intensity is what scared me, back in the kitchen. I haven't felt that kind of passion, that fire in forever."

"I'm sorry." He raises his eyes to meet hers, and right away his hopeful heart squeezes. It doesn't seem to matter how hard he fights it, he adores her. Adores the shades of brown and green in her eyes, the little half-moon creases at the corners of her mouth when she smiles. He adores her cotton candy hair and the way her hand feels so right in his.

"You've seen how attracted I am to you," she sighs, picking up her mug. "But you've also seen how much this scares me. The moment you touched my butt... that forward sexual contact... I froze."

"I got carried away."

She shakes her head. "No, I wanted it. I wanted you. My hands were hardly shy." Her gaze drops to his chest. "But I guess I panicked."

He picks up his own mug. The ceramic is now cool against his sweltering palm. "I understand, and I'm not going to push you. Whatever you need me for I'm more than willing to give."

"Thank you." She takes a sip, her eyebrows creasing the

moment the cold chocolate touches her lips. "I wasn't sure if it even made sense."

"It does. I mean, I'd be lying if I said this didn't scare the shit out of me too."

She frowns and smiles at the same time, "It scares you?"

Warning bells ring in the back of his mind. She just opened her heart and told him about her nightmarish possessive ex. Admitting he's in real danger of falling in love with her—which might also be a lie because he strongly suspects he's already fallen—is thin ice.

"In the best possible way." He settles on the best answer he can think of. It's also the truth. "You know, when we first met it was the same week as my old band broke up, and the same night I was stood up. And then you came into my life, purple-haired and so beautiful you made me breathless."

"Ah," she smiles. "I was wondering when you'd finally make a comment about how I look. So far all we've done is argue your ranking and talk about how handsome you are."

His cheeks heat as he gives an awkward laugh. "Mémé always told me not to talk about a woman's looks unless you're absolutely sure she gives a shit about your opinion, and even then, proceed with caution."

"She sounds like a wise woman." Jordan chuckles. "But for the record, your opinion is worth a whole heap of shit."

"Then I thought you were beautiful even before you came over to sit with me. I saw you walking across the room and the sight of you…" He suddenly grows self-conscious. There is that hopeless romantic streak in him, running away with himself.

"What about the sight of me?" She says gently.

Her eyes drop a little lower to his nose. He's definitely doing the dorky crinkle-nose smile. Goddammit.

"Go on." She turns to face him, hitching her knees up onto the couch and bracing her elbow against the back. "Rank me. Do your worst."

"From one to ten?"

"Yup. And be honest. I've played cello since I was eleven years old, so I can take criticism."

"Alright." He makes a show of scrutinizing her features, all the while trying to think of how to phrase his answer. But he can't think of anything witty or poetic enough to do her justice. "Honestly, I can't."

She looks a little disappointed, her shoulders deflating an inch as she settles against the back of the couch.

"I don't even think I can put your beauty into words, let alone numbers."

Her breath catches a little before she reaches out to gently pat his arm. "You're so smooth."

"Actually, I'm kind of hairy."

The little snort of laughter she gives at his weak joke is better than anything he could ever ask for. "I know."

"Oh yeah?"

She nods, biting back a smile. "The other day in rehearsals, you lifted up your shirt to wipe your face and I saw your stomach is pretty hairy. Not to mention your shirt necklines have been getting progressively lower since I met you."

Instinctively he raises a hand to the top of his chest. She's right. There's a good expanse of chest hair on display above the black cotton of his t-shirt. Her eyes follow the movements of his fingers as he rasps his hand across his bare skin. "It's not completely accidental."

"Were you trying to seduce me via the medium of chest hair, Monsieur?"

He leans a little closer, mirroring the way her elbow forms a bracket between her temple and the back of the couch. "Since the moment I met you."

F uck taking it slow.

She's done with checking over her shoulder. Done with holding back until she's sure she's safe. She wants him.

Jordan's heart races as she pushes forward, her lips colliding with Étienne's with a force which surprises them both. But once the initial gasps of disbelief have faded, kissing him is as natural and as necessary as breathing. He tastes sweet, chocolate and marshmallows but the heat with which he kisses her is anything but.

This time she doesn't panic. He isn't Danny. He's nothing like him. Étienne is every bit as passionate and she burns just as brightly for him, but he's gentle, considerate. When he kisses her, it isn't like he's stealing her heart and soul the way Danny would. No. He's giving her his.

She needs more, more of that heat, more of him. Her whole body moves toward his, maneuvering until she straddles his hips and breaks their kiss long enough to gasp, "Is this okay?"

He nods instead of speaking, as if unwilling to spend another moment not kissing her. It's perfect, but there's still some part of her that worries she'll forget herself if he touches her.

Gently, she threads her fingers through his and pins his arms up and over his head, against the back of the couch. A deep, longing moan escapes his lips, and he seems all too happy to sit there held beneath her. Okay, he likes that. She sinks her teeth into his lower lip, coaxing another wanton sigh.

"Still okay?" she whispers against his lips.

"God, yes."

Jordan sits upright, her pulse shaking her vision as she lifts her shirt up over her head. She sits back and watches the way his eyes scour her figure, how his lips part to let in hard-won breaths. She hasn't even taken off her bra yet and she can tell from the way his eyelids hang that he's already lust-drunk. It's just a simple black bra, nothing fancy, but he doesn't seem to care. He keeps his hands up where she can see them, palms facing her in a sign of surrender.

She's completely in control, and that's exactly what she needs.

Tingles shoot through her, pooling between her thighs as she reaches behind to unhook her bra. His eyes immediately go to her chest, his top teeth sinking into his lower lip as he waits.

A slight flutter of nerves rolls through her as she pulls away the molded cups of her bra, letting her breasts hang free. They're large and heavy, ridged with faded silver stretch marks, and hang almost to her stomach while she's sitting like this. No matter how often she repeats mantras about loving the skin she's in, there's always a voice in the back of her mind, chastising her for something completely beyond her control.

"Fuck," Étienne breathes. "You're so beautiful." His chest rises and falls, as he moistens his lips with the tip of his tongue. "So beautiful."

She lets her hands drop lower, to the waistband of his jeans. His erection is hard to miss, straining against black denim, thick and sturdy like the rest of him. Part of her longs to touch him there, to pleasure him and watch him come undone, but another, far louder part wants to take things slow, to take pleasure for herself. She'd tried rushing things at the wedding, but Étienne is definitely something to be savored.

Pushing her hands beneath the hem of his shirt, she strokes the soft, bristled slope of his stomach, her mouth curling into a smile along with his.

Her breath catches in her throat as she speaks. "I want to see you too."

Eyes half-lidded, Étienne pulls off his shirt and tosses it onto the floor behind her. The sight of him sends a flood of heat and desire coursing through her body. He's everything she imagined, sturdy but soft, compact yet thick. His chest and stomach are dusted with dark hair, and it's impossible not to reach out and touch him. She runs a hand down the valley in the center of his chest, over the hill of his stomach, relishing the way his body bows to her touch. He's perfect.

Leaning forward, she presses her bare chest to his as she kisses him deeply.

"Do you want to head to the bedroom?" he whispers. There's a tremble in his voice, which sounds like hope, nerves, and arousal.

She's never wanted anything more.

A moment of hesitation from her gives Étienne pause. The last thing he wants to do is push her into something she doesn't really want, especially after what she has told him.

"It's okay if not," he assures her. "If this is all we ever do, then I'm more than happy—"

"I want to," she says, threading her fingers through his once more. The dark look in her eyes sends bolts of anticipation to his cock. When she pinned his hands against the back of the couch, he almost came right there and then. It had taken monumental self-control to slow down.

She climbs off him and waits while he stands. When they're eye-to-eye she kisses him again, her fingertips lightly tracing the curve of his jaw. "I want you," she tells him.

"I want you too." He leads her to the back of his apartment, to his bedroom. It's his favorite room, the one where he's happy to spend money on comforts. Jordan's eyes drift to the big monstera plant standing by the window, and then over the framed vinyl records on his walls. He thanks every force in the universe that he actually made his bed using his favorite thick white cotton sheets that morning.

He'd be lying if he said he wasn't nervous, and he can tell she is too. She stands there, topless and perfect, one arm across her chest as she rests her hand on the opposite shoulder. A craving resonates in the back of his throat, painfully close to articulation, but tethered by uncertainty.

Thankfully, she takes the lead. She turns to him and unbuttons her jeans, pulling them down over her wide hips and thick, dimpled thighs until she stands in nothing but her dark blue panties. The sight of her damn near winds him. He could spend hours kissing every part of her. Perhaps tonight he'll get to.

"Your turn," she says.

He obeys, unbuckling his belt and unfastening his jeans. As he inches them down, her eyes lower to the bulge of his erection straining against his boxers. She has to know. She has to know how gorgeous she is, how much he loves having her tell him what to do. And perhaps, if he did tell her what he was thinking, what he desperately wants to ask her, it would be a comfort for her. If he was tied down and she was in complete control of his pleasure and hers…

"Is something wrong?" Her throat bobs as she swallows hard. Lowering her arm, she reveals her breasts again, and his cock twitches at the sight of her nipples, so hard and flushed pink.

She trusts him, and it's time he returned the favor.

"Yeah… um…" His mouth is so dry he can barely draw breath. "I like to be tied up."

Okay, it came out a little blunter than he had rehearsed.

She stares at him, a small furrow forming between her eyebrows. "How do you mean?"

"To the bed." He drags the air into his lungs. She's going to run for the hills at any moment. "I'm sorry. I don't really tell people about it until we've been together for a while, but I thought maybe, if you were completely in control, you'd feel more comfortable—"

"Let's do it." The commanding tone to her voice almost floors him. "What do I tie you up with?"

Well, shit.

"Okay." His heart races as he turns to his nightstand and takes out the black leather straps for his wrists and ankles. She watches him as he secures a strap to each of the four corners of his bed, looping them around the bedframe and ensuring they're tight. As he fastens the buckle on the last one, she comes up behind him, pressing her body against his. Her hand slowly follows the curve of his ass as her breath blows hot against the back of his neck. Goosebumps raise on his forearms and thighs.

"Tell me everything you want," she whispers.

He's never been more turned on in his life. Slowly, she rakes her nails along the sides of his thighs as she leaves lingering kisses on his shoulders.

"God," he shivers at her touch. "I want you to tie me down and use me to get yourself off."

"Do you want me to sit on your face?"

He leans back into her touch. "Yes. Please."

"And ride your cock when I'm done."

"Yes." The world tilts around them as the blood rushes from his head and into his boxers. He nods.

"Do you have condoms?"

"Bedside table," he manages to say.

She kisses his neck as she hooks her thumbs beneath the waistband of his boxers and tugs them down to his knees.

"Lie down," she commands.

He does as he's told, shaking off his boxers and climbing onto the bed. His body trembles as he spreads his arms and legs, each limb pointing toward a corner of the bed. His cock stands firm, throbbing as she takes up the first strap.

"Tell me if it's too much?" She says, as if this whole thing was her idea.

"I will," he assures her. "You won't hurt me."

"How do I make this as good as possible for you?"

Her concern touches him. "Just… whatever feels good for you. I'm yours."

"Okay." She leans down to kiss him, and with his free hand he reaches over to gently caress her cheek. Before she breaks away, she sucks his lower lip between hers, grazing it with her teeth. Her kisses steal his breath, and he can't help but moan against her lips.

When she returns her attention to the binding, she rakes a heavy-lidded gaze over his body. "You're mine."

H er breath trembles as she secures the final strap around Étienne's wrist and stands at the foot of the bed. But it isn't fear. His chest rises and falls with his shallow breaths, and his cock twitches in anticipation, a clear bead of precum rolling down his shaft.

It isn't at all how she pictured the evening going when she kissed him at the gas station, but now that they're here she wouldn't have it any other way. She has never done anything like this before. Perhaps it shouldn't feel as natural as it does; it's exactly what she needs.

Stepping around the bed to where he can see her fully, she pulls off her underwear. The lust in his eyes as he gazes upon her is enough to make her lightheaded. His fingers curl and flex, and he moans as though regretting his decision to be tied up so he can't touch her.

"Please," he whispers, his voice rough. "Let me taste you."

"Patience," she tells him.

A muscle in his cheek leaps as he nods. First, she wants to explore his body more. Carefully, she climbs onto the bed, straddling one of his thick, hairy thighs. Her pussy aches with need as she puts her weight on her hands and knees and licks the hard pink bud of his nipple.

"Oh, God," he hisses, pressing his head back against his pillow.

"You're sensitive here aren't you," she smiles, circling his nipple with her fingertip.

He bites his lip as he nods, and a dark pink blush spreads across his cheeks.

His cock is hard against her soft stomach, the heat of his arousal almost too tempting. But ever since she first saw his handsome face, she's wanted to sit on it. As she shifts her weight to the other side so she can give both his nipples her attention, he groans as her body slides against his cock.

Another broken cry escapes his lips as she takes his nipple gently between her teeth and flicks it with the tip of her tongue.

Those sexy grunts and heavy breaths he takes while singing are nothing compared to those he makes when he's truly aroused. With every gasp and whimper her pussy throbs, growing wetter and more desperate for relief. As she continues to tease him, she grinds herself against his sturdy thigh, every roll of her hips sending spikes of pleasure shooting through her.

"God yes," he whispers, craning his neck to watch her.

She kisses him lower, following the dark trail of hair over his belly, until she sits upright.

"I want you to make me come," she tells him, her heart fluttering at the sight of him so turned on. His chest and stomach are flushed too, and the head of his straining cock is dark pink and glistening.

His throat twitches as he swallows. "I'll do anything you want me to."

Standing, she makes her way to the head of the bed, tracing the outline of his side with her fingertips, making him squirm. She climbs up to kneel beside his bicep, watching the way his body shudders with anticipation.

She's never done this, and it takes a moment for her to figure out the position. Her short legs are an advantage as she kneels with her back to the headboard. This way she can see his body, pleasure him while he goes down on her.

"Tell me if I'm hurting you." Her voice shakes a little as she shifts into position.

Étienne wastes no time. No sooner is her pussy above his lips than he's licking her. Pleasure rolls through her body, curling her toes and arching her back. It's so different from lying down, the taboo heightening every sensation as he licks and sucks her clit.

"Oh fuck," she gasps, fighting for balance as her thighs tremble.

He licks her slowly, exploring her with his tongue. Her back bows he traces the lips of her pussy, savoring every moment of her pleasure.

She reaches down and parts her folds, fully exposing her clit to him, pressing down harder against his eager tongue. She's completely in control, and he's more than willing to do exactly as she wants him to do.

She rewards him by leaning forward and returning her attention to his nipples, pinching them between her thumbs and middle fingers, and using her index fingers to tease them. His moan vibrates against her pussy. His toes curl as she rolls her hips, the friction of his beard against her slick, kiss-swollen skin coaxing out a cry of her own.

Reaching down once more, she parts her folds again, rubbing her clit in time with his licks, her orgasm building, tightening like a coil deep within her until she comes, shattering on top of him as it tears through her body. Her thighs tremble as pulse after pulse of pleasure ravages her, bowing her double as he licks and licks.

A moment later and it's too much, her body too sensitive

to his touch, so she leans forward, lifting her hips away from him as he gasps, "God, you taste incredible."

She maneuvers round to face him, sitting astride his stomach as she kisses him. The taste of her on his lips sends a rolling ache through her body.

"Thank you," she whispers, the aftershock tremors of her pleasure still pulsing faintly between her thighs.

"No, thank *you*."

"Are you okay?" She asks, cupping his face in her hands. He's so beautiful, his cheeks flushed pink, his lips parted.

He raises his head as much as he can, kissing her back. "Perfect," he practically growls. "We can do this all night if you want it."

She runs her hands over his chest, up toward his biceps. Étienne sucks in a breath through his teeth, his chest rising as he fixes her in a dark-eyed stare.

"I want to fuck you." The words leave her before she can stop them.

His chest drops as his breath escapes him. "Fuck, yes."

She leans over him, reaching toward his bedside drawer. Inside, tucked beside his underwear is an unopened box of condoms, a half-empty bottle of lube, and a blue rubber cock ring with a small vibrator attached.

"Oh?" She smiles, pulling out the ring. "Can we use this?"

He nods eagerly. "Whatever you want."

Sinking her teeth into her lip, she checks the expiry on the condoms, and satisfied, opens the box and tears one of the packets from the strip. She shuffles down his body, letting his erection brush against her ass as he throws his head back and moans. He's so turned on that even with the cock ring she doubts he'll last long.

He watches her roll the condom onto his dick, his chest and stomach inflating and deflating with every heavy breath. She loves this, being in control of his pleasure, knowing that every touch is on her terms. And though she's never done anything like this before, it feels entirely comfortable.

"I want to come again," she tells him.

"As many times as you like, however you like."

He groans as she fits the ring over his cock, rolling it down until it sits at the base of his shaft. The vibrator attachment is positioned so that when she rides him, it will stimulate her clit. She straddles his hips, lowering herself until the bulbous head of his cock teases her entrance.

"Jordan," he whispers, lifting his head and tensing his belly so he can watch her. But before she takes him, she lets him slide between the lips of her pussy, over her swollen clit. The heat and hardness of him sliding against her pulls another cry from her.

Étienne's lip curls as he watches, transfixed by the sight of his cock being used purely for her pleasure. His voice is husky, dark and breathless. "Does it feel good?"

Jordan nods, letting her eyes close just for a moment. But she can't bear to look away from him. That perfect, devastatingly handsome man is tied there for her pleasure, and loving every minute of it.

Gripping the base of his cock, she flicks the switch on the vibrator and guides him until he's almost entering her, pausing only to relish the look of relief and anticipation on his face. She lowers onto him slowly as his head rolls back, the tendons in his neck thick and straining.

"Fuck," he hisses as his eyes return to her and his chest shakes with a hard, hoarse gasp.

A shiver courses through her body, leaving her breathless.

He feels every bit as good as she thought he would, and despite her hesitation to give in to her desire, he's so completely right.

She leans back, tilting her hips so the vibrator hums against her clit, and reaches behind her to hold on to his thighs.

"That's it," he tells her. "God, look at you. You're so fucking beautiful."

She feels beautiful. As she sets the pace, riding his cock and letting the vibrator pleasure her, she feels like a queen. No, like a *goddess*. The look in his eyes is pure worship and wonder, his fingers flexing with the desire to touch her. He's hers, and she doesn't doubt he'd let her do this to him for the rest of their lives.

"I'm close," he gasps.

She switches pace, riding him slowly, taking him deep, as he groans, denying him his orgasm until she's had hers. From the way he looks at her, his teeth sinking into his lower lip to suppress a smile, that's exactly what he wants.

She frees the vibrator from its attachment on the ring and uses it on herself, sliding down onto his cock and staying there, pleasure travelling down her spine at the sensation of him filling her. Her muscles contract, gripping him as her orgasm builds.

"That's it," Étienne growls. "Oh, fuck I can feel it."

She lets loose, quickening her pace, hard and fast, strumming her clit with the vibrator until she shatters, savage pleasure clawing through her, tearing his name from her lips. He's a second behind her, crying out as he loses control, as he comes undone, legs trembling and fists coiled, wrists staining against the ties. In that moment there is no world beyond them. Just the darkness and stars behind her eyelids, the all-consuming sensation of her pleasure, and the rapturous sounds of his.

When Jordan comes back to earth, the room rotates around her for a moment. She steadies herself, bracing her hands on Étienne's soft stomach.

"Oh, God, Jordan." He gasps staring at the ceiling. His skin is flushed pink and has a faint sheen. "Holy shit."

"Good?" It's all she can manage to say as she grips the base of the condom and climbs off him.

He nods, swallowing hard as he fights to get his breath back. "So good. Perfect."

Jordan smiles and lays down beside him, running her hand through the hair on his chest and belly. He's so warm and soft, and for a moment she considers how lovely it would be to just curl up beside him all night.

THIRTEEN

She's incredible. As Étienne lies there, tethered to the bed waiting for her to return from the bathroom, he wonders how the hell he got so lucky. The evening has been a rollercoaster, soaring highs and tumbling, terrifying lows, and he's completely exhausted and entirely satisfied.

His heart skips when Jordan comes back into the room and lies beside him, stroking his torso and kissing his chest as he watches her eyelids grow heavy.

If he's really honest, all he wants to do is hold her, but for now she keeps him tied. It's fine. He's more than happy to do everything on her terms.

"Thank you for being so open to this," he says. "Part of me thought you were just going to run the hell away from here when I mentioned it."

"Oh, please," she chuckles, dismissing the very idea. She strums her thumb over his sensitive nipple, making him jerk. "As kinks go this is pretty tame."

"Are you disappointed?"

She obviously hears the trepidation in his voice, as she

rolls over and raises onto her elbows. Her eyes dart back and forth over his features. "No. Never. It was perfect." She places a gentle, lingering kiss on his lips. "You're perfect."

She's so beautiful, so intoxicating. The heady scent of her arousal still lingers, captured by the bristles of his beard. He'll happily stay drunk on her forever. "Ditto."

For a moment she gazes down at him, strumming her fingers over his chest, before reaching out to the corner of the bed to untie his arm. The urge to touch her is overwhelming, but he holds back, resting his arm on the pillow as she works on untying the other.

"I'm so glad you turned me down at the wedding," she says.

"Trust me, it was painful to do."

"But things probably wouldn't have worked out this way." She flashes a brief, uncertain smile, firmly rubbing his shoulders with her fingertips. "Would you have let me tie you up then?"

"Probably not. I don't tell people about this unless I completely trust them. I didn't know you. I didn't even know your name." He chuckles contentedly, bringing one arm across his belly. "If you'd left afterwards and told me not to contact you, I would have left the audition as soon as I recognized you."

"Well, that's just another reason for me to be thankful we didn't. But this… this feels right."

"It does. I trust you."

"I trust you too."

He can barely breathe as she lifts his hands from his stomach and guides him, pulling him over gently until he lies on his side, and rests his arm over the valley of her waist. She rolls onto her side, facing him, pressing her lips to his shoulder and nuzzling his neck with the tip of her nose.

Her eyes close as he strokes her back with his fingertips, keeping his touch light but deliberate.

"You feel right," she whispers as she rests her hand on the side of his stomach.

Those words stay with him long after she drifts off to sleep, her warm breath fluttering against his shoulder, because nothing until now has ever felt truer.

The next morning Jordan stands in his kitchen, sipping black instant coffee from a white wolf mug which his mémé bought him at the zoo. Étienne smiles at her over the top of his chipped green National Parks mug for perhaps the billionth time. He's fully aware he has slipped into goofy, love-struck teen mode, but there's nothing he can do about it. He's infatuated beyond redemption.

His body aches deliciously, his wrists and ankles tingling with the memory of the tethers. But the ache in his heart is far more severe. A voice in the back of his mind goads him, telling him he should ask if they'll get to do this again. He wants to, desperately. Hell, he'll do this every day for the rest of his life if she wants to. But he knows it has to be on her terms. He won't do anything to push her or make her uncomfortable.

"So…" Jordan clears her throat and sets her coffee down. "What happens now?"

He chuckles against the rim of his mug. "You read my mind."

She backs up to lean against the cabinets, bracing her

hands on the grey granite countertop. Some primal, feral desire to press his body to hers, to fuck her in the kitchen, claws at him, followed by the perhaps irrational fear that she can actually read his mind.

"I like you," she says firmly. "And I'd like to keep doing this."

His heart cartwheels, but he tries to maintain a veneer of cool. "Neat."

Neat? Fucking neat?

She smiles at him affectionately. "But this can't affect the Vixens in any way, okay? I don't even want them to know about it."

"Okay." He nods, but he can already see Finn's enthusiastic grin. "We'll be the very model of professionalism. I won't breathe a word of it to anyone."

She pushes back from the counter and approaches him, her top teeth grazing her lip. "Thank you."

He surrenders to her whim, stepping back against the pantry door as she pins him in place with her body. She's soft, sweet and gentle until she isn't, gripping his hands with a feral need and holding them back against the cool, smooth door as she kisses him. Bitter black coffee dances on his tongue, the heat of her body just as intoxicating this morning as when she fucked him last night.

He barely knows anything about her, what she does when she isn't a Vixen, her full name, her hobbies beyond music. And yet, he knows every inch of her intimately. He knows the sounds she makes when she comes. He knows she mutters in her sleep, and that beneath the pink dye her hair is mostly grey with stubborn strands of toffee brown.

Her teeth tug his lower lip, sending a thrill of excitement

through his body, as she slides her hands up his wrists and palms, to lace her fingers with his.

There's little point in denying it, he has already completely lost himself to her. He already knows he loves her, but he won't say it, not until she's ready.

Over the course of the following days, the band rehearse like never before in preparation for recording. They sound incredible, with Étienne's voice the perfect complement to their sound. And though outwardly they keep it strictly professional, Jordan can hardly keep her eyes from him. She plays while he sings, every lyric, every note a tribute to them, to whatever beautiful thing it is they share.

A sour flicker of disappointment crosses her heart when Finn tells Étienne his car is fixed, and he won't need to get rides from him, or Jordan anymore. But the bitterness is quickly diluted by amusement as Étienne presents the drummer with his thank you gift. Jordan fights back a smile as Finn enthusiastically unwraps what must be his twentieth Animal from The Muppets t-shirt and pulls Étienne into a rib-crushing embrace. It's a sweet gesture, so sweet she risks forgetting she can't just wrap her arms around Étienne and kiss him whenever she feels like it.

And boy does she ever feel like it.

After practice they drive separately back to his apartment, and she ties him to the bed again and fucks him until they're both breathless. There's just something about it, seeing him helpless and loving every moment of it, watching him come undone only when she allows it, only when she's come as many times as she wants to.

"You're amazing," he pants as she unties him and pulls him to her so he can rest his head between her breasts and wrap his arms around her. "Fucking hell."

She feels amazing. Their first time together was everything she didn't know she needed, but now... now it's everything she craves. With Étienne there's no fear of having control taken from her. She's safe, respected, and she comes harder and more often than she ever has with anyone else.

"You're amazing too," she whispers, smoothing his ruffled hair. "This is amazing. It just keeps getting better."

Leading him through the hallway of his own apartment, she takes him to the shower and gets in beside him. She takes a bar of lemon-scented soap and lathers up her hands before sliding them around his body, exploring every slick curve, kissing his lips all the while.

"I love this," he whispers as his eyes close, blocking out the cascade of water.

"So do I."

She takes a half step toward him, pressing his body to hers. His skin is warm and slippery, his body firm and soft all at once. He never touches her unless she allows it, a habit of his she didn't realize she needed until it was already happening. She trusts him almost completely.

She turns her back to him and pulls her hair over her shoulder. "Would you wash my back?"

"Of course."

Bowing her head, she braces herself for his touch. At the first press of his palms, flat and warm against her shoulder blades, her skin shivers and any apprehension she has flows away with the water. He's gentle, firm, and oh-so-attentive, his soapy hands gliding over her skin. He doesn't go any lower than her back, doesn't try to grab her ass or work his way round to her front.

"Thank you," she smiles as she turns back around and takes the soap from him.

He watches as she washes herself, his throat twitching as she lifts her breasts to clean beneath them, but he never reaches out, never violates their silent agreement.

"What do you do for a living?" she asks as she rinses off. "When you're not singing, I mean."

"Not a whole lot at the moment," he replies. The way his chin dips as he answers makes it seem as though he's embarrassed. "My old band played at things like weddings, parties, events… that kind of stuff, but I've done all kinds. I sold tickets in a movie theater, waited tables. I was a barista for about four hours before they fired me. I was an elf for a mall Santa one year."

She can't help but laugh at the last part. "Wait, seriously?"

He nods, amusement overriding his shame. "Yeah. I had to wear candy striped leggings, shoes with bells on. I had to shave my beard." His nose crinkles. "They put blusher on my cheeks and drew freckles on me."

"And I bet you rocked it."

"Oh absolutely. I was the hottest piece of ass at the North Pole." He quirks his eyebrows up and chuckles at his own joke along with her. "What about you?"

"Nothing that exciting," she says, lathering her hair with his 3-in-1 shampoo and breathing in the cool masculine scent. "I temp at offices, filing, data entry, answering phones. It pays the bills, but it means I can be flexible and fit my hours around Vixens practice."

It also makes her harder to track down. Back when she

first started temping, part of the appeal was that there was less risk of Danny bumping into her and knowing where she worked. She could switch roles whenever she liked.

"And you can quit the moment you go meteoric," Étienne grins as he lathers his own hair.

"What do you mean?"

"It's only a matter of time before Vixen's Wail make it big."

The thought of it scares her as much as it excites her. She grimaces a little.

Étienne laughs. "What?"

"I don't know. Making a living just from music has been my dream for as long as I can remember, but the thought of it, of my passion fading and the only emotions I get from it being resentment or shame when we get bigger and inevitably the criticisms start to come?"

"All artists get criticism. Most of it is because what we do is so subjective."

"So, it wouldn't bother you if someone said you were a bad singer?"

"No, I know I'm a good singer. I might not be to that particular person's taste, but that doesn't mean I'm bad."

She sighs. "I can barely cope with the attention I get now. I could never do what you do."

Étienne shrugs with an effortless confidence. "I just like to be on show, as you can probably tell. When I perform, I do it with the thought that I'm going to get over half the audience wishing they were me, and the others wishing they were fucking me." He laughs before biting his lower lip.

The gesture hollows her chest and sends heat between her thighs. "Do you do that in rehearsals too?"

"No." He raises his arms combing his fingers back

through his hair and rinsing away the suds. "When we're in rehearsals I sing to you."

"So that I wish I was fucking you?"

He grins. "Well, that's a pleasant side effect, but no. I sing to you because it's the only way I can do those beautiful, poetic words justice."

She searches his face for a trace of ridicule, but all she finds is sincerity. "Really?"

"When I was anxious, when I had stage fright, I closed my eyes and pretended you and I were the only people there and it was like this weight lifted from my chest." The cool cockiness fades completely, leaving behind a gentle, heartfelt smile. " When I sing to you it's with my entire heart."

She can't fight the urge to kiss him anymore. As the water cascades over them, she runs her fingers through his hair, kissing him slowly at first, teasing him until the torment becomes too much for her. She only breaks away to tell him, "Put your arms around me."

He does, one arm around her waist, the other around her shoulders, holding her to him with a strength that borders on ferocious.

He's perfect. They're perfect. And in that moment, she knows with all certainty that nothing can ever come between them.

FOURTEEN

A couple of days later Étienne sits at his laptop, determined to find a solution to his never-ending worry. The end of his time with the Vixens is creeping ever closer and he has to figure out what comes after that. He needs a job, even if it's only something part time to tide him over. He has to know that after this he isn't just freefalling through darkness with no idea of when he'll hit the bottom.

The last thing he wants is for Jordan to see what a mess he is.

He clicks on the first job site page which comes up in his web search, one which promises to have over three-hundred thousand jobs in his area. There has to be something.

He types the word 'vocalist' into the search bar and waits. Just a second later a message pops up:

0 results found. Try expanding your search.

Beneath that the featured role of 'Warehouse Operator' is advertised in bold blue letters.

He sighs and changes his search to 'musician', sitting back while the laptop whirs and the screen goes white. That's usually a good sign. It means his pile of garbage laptop actually had something to load.

Vixen's Wail are practicing without him today, working on the songs they don't need him for. By the rough estimate Jordan gave him, they should be done in an hour, and a little while after that she'll be round at his place. He smiles to himself and wipes his palms along his thighs. He'd promised he would make dinner for Jordan tonight and the aromatic scent of his slow-cooked beef bourguignon flooding his apartment makes his mouth water.

She had vetoed his original plan to make spaghetti with marinara, insisting that there was nothing less sexy than a dinner date where they would both be covered in pasta sauce.

"Make something French," she had teased him, nipping his lip with her teeth as she said goodbye at the door. "Something fancy."

He'd spent far too long after that googling French recipes and spent more money than he could strictly afford finding just the right wine and just the right cut of brisket. If he was doing this, he was doing it right and it seems to have paid off. So far it smells incredible. His chest swells with pride as he imagines her reaction. He even made bread for the two of them, albeit in the bread maker which does pretty much everything for him.

Turning back to the laptop however, his heart sinks. There are only a couple of results for musician, and all of them are for music teachers in various schools. He doesn't know the first thing about musical theory, can't tell a semiquaver from a treble clef. As he scrolls to the bottom the meagre results, the advertisement for the warehouse operator job flashes at him again.

He sighs heavily and tries various new searches; 'singer', 'entertainer', 'backstage staff', 'music shop clerk'. As each results page loads his frustration grows, his chest tightens, and his heart and hope sink further.

His family warned him so many years ago that he might have to someday give up his dream. They tried to be practical, to speak plainly about how small the chances of making it big actually were. He just refused to believe them. Acknowledging they were right all along, even if only to himself for now, is crushing. But there's more to life than dreams.

Glancing up at the picture of his mémé and grandaddy, he lets out a breath.

If he wants the kind of love they had, he has no choice but to let go, to stop clinging to the hope that he can make a living with his music. He has to step up and take whatever job he can. There's no shame in it.

Certainty doesn't make it any less devastating.

He fires off his resume to the warehouse company and sits back, running his palms over the top of his head. It stings, but it's what he has to do, no matter how much his heart protests. He sends off a few more applications, each one just as painful as the first.

A knock at the door makes his pulse race. Jumping up to answer it, he curses himself for not changing clothes earlier. He's rarely sloppily dressed, but he had wanted to fancy up a little for her. But when he opens the door none of it matters.

"Hi," she beams. Her pink hair is pulled up in a messy ponytail, a little damp from a day spent in the sweltering rehearsal room. She's bundled up in a thick, black puffer jacket, her breath bursting from her chattering lips in plumes. She's gorgeous, and the sight of her lessens the blow of giving up his dream. Her eyes widen. "Holy shit it smells good in here."

"Beef bourguignon," Étienne grins, stepping back to let her in and get her out of the cold. That bubble of pride returns as she bustles into his hallway, carrying her cello case with her. These days, whenever she comes into his apartment, he isn't afraid of what she'll think, isn't nervous about the less than luxurious furnishings. He's just grateful she's there at all.

All of their meetings have been at his place. It will take some time before she's comfortable enough to invite him to hers, and that's fine. He enjoys having her there, even if it does make the times she's gone all the more lonely.

"I hope you don't mind me bringing my cello." She says, setting it down opposite the couch. "It's a little too cold out there to leave it in the car. The wood can warp."

"Not at all." He smiles and waits for her to take off her jacket.

Inch by inch she reveals a stonewashed grey tank top with the word "heck" emblazoned across it in white gothic lettering. Before she has even pulled the zipper down to the bottom, she turns to face him, her eyes dropping to his lips. He doesn't hesitate, closing the space between them in the span of a heartbeat.

As soon as her lips touch his, he's home, tiny fires bursting beneath the surface of his skin as she sinks into him, slipping her tongue between his lips. He tastes lemonade on her lips, sweet and fresh, and it takes all his willpower to keep his hands at his sides. The last thing he wants is to rush her.

But she touches him, one hand resting in the valley in

the center of his chest, her other arm wrapped around his waist.

When she breaks away, she leaves them both breathless. "I missed you."

"I missed you too." He closes his eyes as she presses her forehead to his. "How was practice?"

"Not the same without you."

His battered ego takes some solace from that. The corners of his mouth lift as he gives a breathy chuckle. "Fewer distractions though."

"I like when you distract me." She smiles and takes his hand in hers, lacing their fingers together. Slowly she raises his hand to the bare expanse of skin above the hem of her shirt and places it above her heart.

Perhaps it's the sensation of touching her, or the steady thrum of her heart beneath his fingertips, but all at once his vision blurs behind a veil of tears. He closes his eyes, unwilling to let them fall, unwilling to let her even suspect for one moment that his heart is secretly breaking. Because if they have a future, this is most likely it. She would continue to live the dream for them both, while he could only watch from the sidelines.

Of course, he would support her. He would burst with pride knowing that she was his, hearing the beauty she created with her instrument. But he would no longer be part of that world with her. He would be washed up, a has-been who never really was.

"It smells so good in here," she repeats, inhaling the scent of his cooking. "I'm starved."

"Alright." He takes her coat and turns toward the kitchen, wiping his eyes on his forearm. "Take a seat."

This is hot.

Having Étienne cook for her, watching the pride he takes as he ladles the steaming beef stew from a Dutch oven into a bowl, and butters thick slices of fresh, warm bread, is almost enough to convince her to skip dinner and get straight to bed. Talk about a competency boner.

He rolls up the sleeves on his black shirt, which fits snug against his sturdy frame, displaying every glorious curve of his body. Jordan fights back the urge to sigh, squeezing her thighs together to silence some of her impatient need.

She can't take her eyes from him as he carries the bowls toward her from the kitchen, a white tea towel thrown over his shoulder as the sinews in his forearms twitch.

"Bon Appétit," he announces as he sets the steaming bowls on the table and heads back to the kitchen, emerging once more with a wooden chopping board topped with the sliced, buttered bread.

"This is amazing," she tells him, sitting on the edge of the couch. "You're amazing."

He lights a cluster of candles on a flat piece of grey slate in the center of the coffee table and switches off the overhead lights, his pleased grin making her smile. He arches an eyebrow as he pours her a glass of merlot from a bottle with a monkey on the label. "Is this fancy enough?"

"So fancy. Just like Paris."

"You've been there?"

She shrugs a shoulder. "I've seen the Aristocats twice."

He gives a playful grin and heads back into the kitchen, leaving her to side-eye the mushrooms swimming in the broth. There's so much satisfaction and hope in his eyes as he returns to the living room carrying his own bowl that she doesn't have the heart to tell him she can't stand them. "Thank you."

"It's my pleasure," he says as he sits beside her, balancing the bowl on his knees. "I'm sorry I don't have a dining table or anything."

Jordan sips the stew from her spoon and sighs as her mouth floods with the delicious, rich taste of red meat and the slightest hint of wine. Even the mushrooms taste good if she ignores the texture. "Oh, God. Étienne, it's perfect."

He smiles when she says his name and her heart smiles with him. It seems so silly now that she ever doubted they could work. This man, who does everything he can to make her comfortable and safe, who cooks for her, who she doesn't even mind eating mushrooms for. Not to mention that she's absolutely mesmerized by his looks. Those cool blue eyes, his soft, full lips, the chest hair. He's perfect in every way.

She knows she should be suspicious of that, but she's too damned love-drunk to care. Dipping her bread into her bowl, she frowns. That phrase came to her mind so easily, but it can't be love. Not so soon. Lust, certainly. Her libido practically hurls her toward him every time she lays eyes on him.

Étienne swallows and clears his throat. "They say good food kills conversation. I'm taking this as a good sign."

"It's a very good sign," she says. "You're a wonderful cook."

"Thank you."

They continue to eat in appreciative silence, until she finishes her meal and sets her bowl down on the table. It's hard not to watch him while he eats; the flex of his jaw, the undulation of his throat. When he finishes, he places his bowl beside hers, wiping his palms along the length of his thick thighs, an innocent enough gesture, but one which has her longing to take him back to his bedroom yet again.

"Did you have a good day?" She asks, desperate for a distraction.

He turns his face away and his jaw twitches as though he's holding something back. With a long exhale he reaches up to rub the back of his neck. "It was okay."

"Just okay?"

"Just… I don't know." He slumps back against the cushions of the couch before his gaze returns to her. "It's better now."

"Mine too."

"Can I ask a favor? It might be a little weird."

She chuckles. "I like weird."

"Would you…" He sighs. "Would you play for me?"

Okay, that she wasn't expecting. "Uh…sure?"

"You don't have to. I just…" He shakes his head and looks away from her, the tips of his ears turning red. "It's soothing. I love listening to you play."

How can she refuse? A smile pulls at her lips as she stands and picks up her case. She glances around the room. "Do you have a chair I can sit on?"

"Oh, yes." He jumps up and heads back into the kitchen, appearing a moment later with a wooden dining chair. She steps back as he places it in front of her, wiping off the seat with the tea towel. "Sorry. Is that okay? I use it to reach the top shelves. I don't have another."

"It's perfect." She sits and unfastens the black cello case, lifting the instrument from its crimson velvet bed and placing it between her knees.

As she tightens her bow and checks the tuning, Étienne returns to the couch. He sits, thighs parted, bathed in flickering candlelight, watching her intently. She has played countless times, in front of so many people, their faces are a blur now, but this time she's nervous. Not because she thinks he'll judge her, but because sitting here before him, she's stripped bare. With his smoldering good looks, it's as though she's playing for the devil himself, only she wants nothing more for him than to win her soul. "What should I play?"

"Anything," he says gently. "Your favorite song or…"

"A Vixens song?"

He nods. "Whatever you like."

She pauses a moment, chewing her lip, her throat drying out as he strokes his thigh again. "Okay." She pulls in a breath and positions the fingers of her left hand on the instrument's neck, ready to play. "This is the song we worked on today. It makes me think of you."

She closes her eyes, placing her bow on the strings and pulling a sonorous moan from the instrument. The song is almost second nature to her now, long hours spent practicing paying off as she conjures melody and magic from wood and wire. As she plays, she pictures him lying beside her, in those moments when they're both spent. Those moments when they are surrendered entirely to each other, nothing hidden, nothing held back. When she reaches the final chorus and switches to a higher key, the hairs on her arms bristle and her chest tightens.

As the song ends, she opens her eyes again and the sight of him steals her breath all together. The intensity in those heavy-lidded eyes burns through her. "Was that okay?"

"Beautiful."

Her heart swells at his praise, but the pleasure quickly fades as tears in his eyes glimmer in the candlelight. "What's wrong?" She sets the cello back in its case and hurries back to his side. Settling on the couch she twists her body to face him, curling her hand around his as it rests on his thigh. "Étienne, talk to me."

He sighs and stares ahead, steadfastly refusing to look at her. "What would you have done if things didn't work out with the Vixens?" he asks, quietly.

"What do you mean?"

He pulls in a breath. "Say, if the Vixens split, what would you do? Would you look for another band?"

"I don't know. There aren't many bands who have space for a cellist."

He chuckles lightly. "I suppose I'm at the other end of that. Plenty of bands need vocalists, but there are so many people who can sing—"

"Not like you."

He turns to face her, his blue eyes glossy as they scan her face. "I used to think so too, but what if we're wrong?"

"We aren't. You know it, I know it. Finn and Mia both know it. Our fans are already in love with you."

"Yeah, well..." He draws an invisible line down the center of his thigh with his thumb, tracing it over and over. "They haven't heard me yet."

"And when they do, they'll just love you more, like I—" She catches herself, the voice in the back of her mind scolding her for jumping in too soon. "Like I said, there aren't many people with your talent."

"Talented people give up their dreams all the time. There's nothing wrong with it. We can't all make it. I need to be practical."

"Hey," she reaches out, splaying her fingers on the side of his jaw which is hidden from her, and turning his face gently toward her. Unable to stand the pain in his eyes, she leans forward and kisses his lips, his cheeks, the tip of his nose and the crease between his eyebrows. "Don't give up."

He exhales hard, his lips parting. "Would you still want me if I wasn't a musician?"

"Every moment of every day. Étienne, I wanted you from the moment I laid eyes on you, even before I heard your voice." Her own vision blurs as fire crackles beneath the surface of her skin. "But you aren't giving up. I got lucky with the Vixens and you'll get your break too. Finn knows everybody. I'm sure if you speak to him and ask him to put some feelers out, he'll know someone who knows someone looking for a singer."

A corner of his mouth lifts slightly as he leans into her touch. The warm rasp of his beard against her palms sends goosebumps across her skin. "Thank you."

Leaning forward, she rests her other hand on the curve of his stomach and brushes her lips against his. "You're perfect."

A low moan breezes through his chest as he submits to her, his lips caressing hers with such desperate longing. "And you're incredible," he whispers. "Thank you for playing for me. It really was beautiful." He chuckles. "That song reminds you of me?"

"Everything beautiful does lately," she says, raising his fingers to her lips and pressing a gentle kiss to the pads of his fingertips.

"What's it called?"

Her breath staggers from her as she shuffles toward him, nestling against his body so she can rest her head on his chest. The steady beat of his heart throbs against her cheek.

"*I'm Yours.*"

FIFTEEN

A week later, Étienne stands before the mic in the center of a recording studio. His phone vibrates in his pocket, but he doesn't bother to check it. It's either a rejection from a job he didn't truly want, or a text from Dan.

The most recent set of messages he's gotten from the guitarist are at least a little more polite than they had been, but still every bit as persistent. He'll deal with them another time. Not today. He hands the phone off to Finn through the recording room door and gets ready for another run-through of the track. The studio's photographer tiptoes to the other side of the room and snaps another shot.

"That last one was awesome," Mia assures him. She's dressed in her whole goth-queen attire again, fully in the roll of the vampiric siren of the night. Her painted black lips draw back to reveal a perfect, dazzling smile. "Just a little more power on the *you will be mine, creature divine* line."

The camera flashes again and the photographer gives a thumbs up before heading out the door.

Étienne nods and bounces on the spot a little, psyching

himself up. He has already sung the line ten times, giving it more power than he thought he was capable of with each new take. But Mia pushes him harder, just like he wants her to.

The rest of the band finished recording their parts that morning, and now stand watching the vocalists on the other side of the observation window.

Lifting the neck of his t-shirt, he dabs the sweat from his brow. He can't help but smile at the thought of Jordan watching him on the other side of the glass, looking at his body and craving him the way he constantly craves her.

He chances a glance over and sure enough, she's there, biting her lip as her gaze trails over him. She makes his heart flutter. Finn stands beside her, the big guy's forehead creased in concentration as he replays parts of the track though a pair of big, red headphones. He leans over and whispers something in Jordan's ear which switches her look from sultry seduction to radiant laughter in a matter of seconds.

The way she tucks her hair behind her ear is hypnotic, the way she steals one last glance at Étienne before turning her attention back to the rest of the band makes his heart soar.

Étienne has never made a secret of the fact he knows how attractive he is, but even with his confidence, he has no idea how he got quite this lucky. Jordan is funny, smart, talented and beautiful. She fucks him like she just heard that the world is ending, and all he can do is lie there and take it and wish it would go on forever. It's everything he's ever wanted. *She* is everything he's ever wanted. He's in love with every part of her.

"You ready to go again?" Mia asks.

"Yeah."

He tears his gaze from Jordan, only to be met with the vocalist's wry smile.

"You sure you don't need a minute?" Mia grins.

"I'm sure."

"You look a little flushed."

Fuck. He can feel the heat creeping up his neck and over his cheeks. "Just hot. I'm fine. Let's go."

Finn's smug grin burns bright beside her as Mia and Étienne break into song again, both of them putting their entire soul into every note. Jordan stares through the glass watching them sing, refusing to look at the drummer.

"I take it it's going well?" He says it quietly, lightly. She can *hear* him smiling.

She doesn't tear her eyes from the recording room. "How do they sound?"

Of course, she knows Finn won't be satisfied by her weak attempt at a diversion. She and Étienne have been caught eye-fucking each other more than once, even before they were actually fucking.

"Just as long as you're happy and being safe," Finn says.

Jordan's head whips round to glare at him. "Are you serious?"

The drummer shrugs. "I care about you both and I don't want to see either of you get hurt."

"Right, but I'm three years older than you. You can't big brother me."

"I'm just saying—"

"At least I don't go around fucking strange women in the woods because they complement my drumkit."

Finn fixes her with a hard stare, and for a moment she panics that she's overstepped the line. But his stern façade crumbles as a snort of laughter bursts from him.

"Fair." He sweeps his hand back through his hair and leans back in his chair. "But I'm not hearing you deny anything, so…?"

The rest of the band stare at her, expectant smiles hidden beneath a flimsy mirage of minding their own business. How they managed to assemble the seven least subtle musicians in the world she'll never truly understand.

"Not a word," Jordan sighs. "Any of you. We're supposed to be keeping it private. Did Étienne tell you?"

Finn shrugs and shakes his head. "He didn't need to."

"He's pretty hot though," the keyboardist, Liz grins. "Thick thighs too. I bet he's like a jackhammer in the edroom—" She's cut short as Anya jabs an elbow into her ribs.

Jordan releases a long sigh and fires a glare at Finn.

"Oh, they all knew anyway," he shrugs. "It really is kind of hard to miss."

Jordan's heart plummets as she glances around her band-mates. "Are you for real?"

"Yeah…" Liz shrugs, collecting her long brown hair in one hand and pulling it over her shoulder, "We knew you were into him pretty much on the day he auditioned."

"Why do you think I asked you to drive him home?" Finn raises his arms and rests them on the back of his head as he swings back in the chair. "I knew you were both into each other, you just needed a little nudge."

"Fuck this." Jordan sighs and folds her arms over her chest. "I take it back. You're more like a meddlesome mother than a big brother."

The drummer's chest shakes as he chuckles. "But I was

right though. And the two of you can't keep your eyes off each other. So… *thank you Finn.*"

Her vision loses focus as her heart stumbles. "Shit. I thought we were subtle."

"You absolutely were not." Finn laughs.

"I can't do it, can I? I need to break it off and it's going to be Danny all over again."

"Jord…"

She tries to swallow as her throat closes. "I promised I would never date another band member and now—"

Finn pulls himself to his feet and gathers her against him. At once she's safe, shielded and grounded, in the arms of her friend. "Hey," he soothes her. "No matter what happens we've got your back, always."

She pulls back a little so her words aren't muffled against him. "But you remember what happened with Danny. You remember how close we came to losing everything because of him?"

"But we didn't. And we're stronger for it." Finn glances down at her, then pulls back so he can hold her at arm's length. "Do you really think Étienne is anything like Danny?"

"I don't know—"

"Jordo." Finn shakes his head a little. "They couldn't be any more different. I wouldn't have left you alone with him unless I was absolutely sure about him."

She glances out of the corner of her eye. Étienne sings into his mic, inaudible past the recording room's soundproof walls. His hands are splayed at either side of his headphones, his eyes screwed tight as he sings his heart out. As he sings for her.

Just the sight of him gives her a warm, glowing feeling.

Not a destructive, chaotic fire like she felt with Danny, but one that burns just as hot and bright, lasting an eternity. Like starlight.

He's buzzing after the recording. It's the last time he'll see the whole band until the day before the festival. The others have the rest of the album to record without him. But he doesn't feel sad. He's elated, and the music is only part of it.

As they leave the studio, Jordan stays behind talking to Finn in the parking lot. Étienne lingers out of earshot, meticulously checking over his perfectly fine car, tying his already fastened shoes, checking his phone and dismissing texts from Dan without even reading them. Anything to buy him an extra few seconds so he can speak with Jordan alone.

He's about to give up when she holds open her arms and Finn steps into her embrace. Her arms stretch around his broad, brawny torso, her head nestled against his chest.

A slight twinge of jealousy nags at Étienne, a longing for her to trust him that way, to fall into his arms with such ease, but he quickly dismisses it. They're going at her pace, and he loves every moment of it.

"See you tomorrow," she calls over her shoulder to the drummer.

"Bye Jord," he replies before yelling over to Étienne. "Bye Baby Bear."

Étienne waves goodbye as the drummer ambles past his own black van and climbs into the driver's seat of Jordan's car. Weird.

His confusion is quickly forgotten as Jordan heads over and his heart begins to skip.

"I see you've mastered the art of elusive lingering," she mutters with a grin as she approaches.

Her smile is magnetic and infectious. "I'm sorry. I just… I wanted to ask if you have plans tonight."

"I do."

"Ah."

She flashes her smile again, her eyes fixed on his, communicating something silent, a secret between them. The glint in her eye, the way her teeth graze her lower lip, it's impossible to miss her intentions.

Her plans involve absolutely rocking his world.

Disappointment gives way to excitement. His heart kicks up into a boisterous rhythm, and not entirely because of the sex. Just spending time alone with her makes him happy beyond measure. "Oh! Great."

She closes the distance between them in a half-step, "I want to try something a little different tonight."

He swallows hard, his cock already at half-staff. "Of course."

"Alright," she says, heading round to the passenger side of his car. "Finn's taking my car home tonight and Beth is driving his van. So, I need a ride if that's okay?"

"No problem."

His pulse pounds in his ears as he gets into the driver's seat. A plague of possibilities swarm through his mind; perhaps she wants more sex, perhaps she's breaking up with him, perhaps they're going out for dinner first and then sex.

And then she's going to break up with him.

He turns the ignition and his stereo blasts to life, part way through his favorite song, A-ha's *Take on Me*.

His ears flush red as he turns the volume down. "Sorry."

Jordan chuckles beside him. "I like that song."

"*Everybody* likes that song. It's the best song ever written."

She doesn't contradict him or make him feel embarrassed. He clears his throat and shrugs a shoulder. "I sing it on the way to rehearsal to help me warm up."

Her smile broadens. "Well, you have the range for it."

Étienne's heart swells a little at the compliment. She's right, he does have the range. That masterpiece of Norwegian synth-pop spans two and a half octaves and allows him to show off his ability to belt out an E5 and work on his falsetto at the end of the chorus. He fights back the urge to sing as they set off driving, Jordan directing him through the steady stream of traffic. When the next song on his playlist starts and it's yet more 80's pop, he can feel the searing heat of Jordan's side-eyeing glance.

"What?" he asks.

"Nothing," she shrugs, turning her attention back to the road ahead of them. "I guess we just have a lot to learn about each other still."

It's hard to tell from her tone, whether that's a good thing or not.

He cringes internally, but tries to play it off. "I'm sorry. Wedding singer."

"Don't apologize. Turn left here," Jordan says.

He follows her directions, his fingers curled tight around the steering wheel and sweat prickling his back. The orange glow of overhead streetlights cuts through the darkness as they drive through the suburbs. The anticipation of what's to come makes him jittery. It's a nice little neighborhood. Nothing too fancy, but quiet and green.

Jordan pulls in a breath. "My place is just up ahead. The one with the blue door."

She points out her house and a wave of excitement rolls over Étienne. This is her home, her sanctuary, and it means a lot that she's inviting him in. Hell, it means the whole world.

The blinkers click as he turns into her driveway, into the space where her car would normally sit. Her porchlight switches on as they pull up, triggered by a motion sensor. Brilliant white light illuminates them, and for the first time he can see her anticipation. She pulls her lower lip between her teeth and the tip of her thumb is red and sore where she has picked at a hangnail.

He turns off the engine and awaits further instruction.

Jordan's breath staggers from her. "So, this is my home."

"Yeah, I guessed." Étienne unbuckles his seatbelt and sits back, his hands on his thighs. "Are you sure about this?"

He sees her turn toward him out of the corner of his eye, her hair swaying over her shoulder, glistening like pink champagne in the light. "Yeah…" She says quietly before repeating herself with a little more certainty. "Yeah. But Étienne, I need you to promise me something before we go in."

His eyes meet hers and the sight of her almost melts him. Worry and hope battle for dominance in his chest. "Anything."

She swallows. "Promise you won't break my heart. That I can keep on trusting you, and you'll never make me regret it."

"Jordan," her name escapes his lips as he curls his fingers to his palm, desperate to touch her. Her gaze drops to his hand. "I'd never," he tells her. "I'll never do anything to hurt you. I promise."

The air in his lungs turns to cement as she reaches out and takes his hand in hers, lifting it from his thigh and slowly bringing it to her cheek. "I believe you."

The sensation of her is addictive. Her skin is soft and warm beneath his knuckles. She leans across the space between them and kisses him gently, her lips lingering on his as he keeps his hand held to her cheek.

When she pulls away, there's just a trace of a smile on her lips. Fragile, fleeting, but it's there. "So, would you like to come in?"

SIXTEEN

Other than Finn, her brother, and her dad, Jordan hasn't had another man in her house since the realtor showed her around. She wrings her hands together as she follows Étienne through the hallway into the living room.

His head is on a swivel, taking in everything he can as she sets her cello down safely. He's fascinated by the taxidermied butterflies and beetles in gilded display cases on her walls.

"Did you make all these?"

"I wish. Actually, these displays come from a sanctuary. When the bugs die naturally the sanctuary sends them off to be mounted like this, and then they're sold to raise funds..." she trails off. "Sorry. It's probably not all that interesting."

"It is," he says without taking his attention from the black and tan exoskeleton of a Hercules beetle. "So, they don't just kill them?"

"No. They live a long and happy buggy life. Well, as long as a normal buggy life, which actually isn't all that long."

"That's good."

His eyes drift over the ornate black framed mirror above

her fireplace and focus on the cabinet of curios she's spent years accumulating.

"These are ammonites, right?" he says.

"Yeah. Those come from Whitby in England, which is also where Bram Stoker wrote Dracula."

She's geeking out, she knows she is, but it's exciting just having somebody there to look over the treasures she's collected. "And that long, skinny stick looking thing at the back is actually the fossilized penis bone of a cave bear. It's about twenty-four thousand years old."

His eyebrows raise. "Well…that's… talk about endurance, huh?"

She laughs, her heart fit to bursting. Having him there is so easy, so natural.

"Your house is super cool," he says, turning to sit on her black leather sofa. His eyes are still wide, still scanning the room. "Like a museum."

Her chest swells with pride. "Thank you."

"I thought you were just a goth on stage. I didn't realize you actually were…"

"I'm a casual goth." She chuckles, standing in front of him. "Does it put you off?"

"No! No not at all." He reclines against the back of the couch, making himself more comfortable. His thick thighs part invitingly, and he gazes up at her, his eyes heavy-lidded and expectant. "Am I here to be your ritual human sacrifice then?"

She shrugs playfully. "Ritual human sacrifices are really more of a Tuesday thing."

He smiles up at her. No matter how much she tells herself to take it slow, she can't help that she's falling for him. No. Not falling.

She's *plummeting*.

Everything about him, his looks, his dorky sense of humor, his confidence, his love of cheesy music, his mismatched mugs and the photos on his walls, the way he never pushes her, his beef bourguignon, that he cares about the lives of bugs… *everything* is perfect. She trusts him, and she needs him to know.

"Are you okay?" he asks gently.

She nods. Her heart flutters against her ribs. "I was thinking, maybe you'd want to have something to eat here with me."

"I'd love that."

"We'll have to order in," she shakes her head in annoyance at herself. "I didn't really think this through a whole lot. I'm sorry. You cooked me such a wonderful meal last time."

"That suits me fine. Anything we do is perfect for me."

She can't keep stalling. The longer she stands there, the more worry etches into his handsome features, deepening the creases between his eyebrows. "I'm kind of nervous."

The crease disappears as his eyebrows raise. "Why?"

"Because…Because I know it's soon and we don't know a whole lot about each other, but I can feel myself falling for you, Étienne." She brings her hands up to her chest, raking her fingernails over the already-raw hangnail. She can't look at him. "When this began, we said it would just be a trial run, but this doesn't feel like a trial. It feels like the real thing."

The air in the living room grows thick and heavy between them. There's no sound but the rapid pulse of her heartbeat in her ears.

"Jordan…" Étienne leans forward and languidly rubs his fingers back and forth over his lips. There's no sound except the coarse hair of his beard rasping against the pads of his fingertips. His gaze is cool and sultry, but the tips of his ears glow red as the corner of his mouth lifts into a smile. "I've been thinking the same."

"Oh, thank fuck."

She's on him in an instant, straddling his hips on the couch as she kisses him, hard and desperate, hungering for him. Every touch of his lips spreads fire across her skin.

"Touch me," she gasps.

"Where?"

She pulls off her shirt and tosses it onto the floor behind her. "Everywhere."

He doesn't hesitate as they kiss again. His palms skim her sides, following the curves of her hips and waist. Unhooking her bra, she sucks in a breath as his hands glide over her stomach, tracing the outskirts of her navel, exploring the softness of her body.

There's no urge to back away, no fear of intimacy. It feels right.

"Jordan." He whispers her name like an incantation, binding her to him.

He fills his hands with her breasts, the firm press of his erection hot against her thigh as he bows his head to kiss every inch of her. The world around them fades as she lifts his shirt to touch his body.

"Do you want to head upstairs?" she asks, as his breath blows warm hot against her neck as his teeth graze her throat.

"God, yes."

"I want you on top of me."

He raises his head to look her in the eyes. "Are you sure?"

"Yes." She's never been more certain of anything. She trusts him, she wants him.

She loves him.

He nods as his throat bobs and his jaw flexes. "Whatever you want."

"I want you."

His throat is tight as she leads him upstairs to her bedroom. He hardly notices the unusual décor anymore, only vaguely aware that one of her bedroom walls is black and her bedsheets are a deep rich purple. Beyond that, the world no longer exists. Or rather it's now composed solely of the woman gazing up at him from the bed.

"Are you sure?" He asks, his voice trembling as the words leave him.

She nods and lies back, lifting her hips so she can wriggle out of her jeans. When they're off she tosses them onto the floor at the side of the bed. "So sure."

He follows her lead, pulling down his jeans, releasing his aching cock from the constricting denim. His stomach muscles tighten as her gaze trails over his body, wanton need darkening her eyes and pebbling her perfect, soft skin.

Every moment away from Jordan is unbearable torture. He climbs onto the bed and makes his way toward her on his hands and knees, kissing the insides of her thighs as he moves into position. He works his way up her body, kissing her stomach, her chest, her breasts, until he's at eye level with her, bracing his weight on his forearms at either side of her head. Slowly, he grinds his hips against hers, sending bolts of pleasure darting through his body.

"Étienne." His name shudders from her lips as she raises her arms to wrap them around his back. She kisses him, slow and deep, the heat of her pussy pulsing against his cock even through their underwear.

His body begs him to fuck her, to tear off her panties, free his dick from his boxers, and thrust into her hard and fast until they're both spent. But he knows what this means. She doesn't want him tied down. She wants him to touch her, she trusts him. And he intends to spend every moment worshipping her body.

She tilts her chin as he kisses down her throat, aching even harder as her moan vibrates beneath his lips. He works lower, kissing her big, beautiful tits, down over the soft cushion of her silver-scarred stomach. She squirms a little as his kisses turn to licks, and her fingers tangle in his hair.

With a grin, he realizes she's gently pushing him lower, and he's more than happy to oblige.

His cock twitches as she lifts her hips and pulls down her underwear, revealing her pussy to him. Her honey-blonde curls are already soaked and god, she smells so fucking good. He helps her pull them down the rest of the way, kissing her ankles as he lets the underwear fall onto the bed.

She's watching him, her chest rising and falling quickly in anticipation. When he's tied up, she likes to tease, to delay his pleasure, and he suspects she enjoys the same for herself. A broken moan escapes her as he holds her gaze and moistens his lips with the tip of his tongue.

He parts his lips and lowers his head, relishing the way her breath catches and her thighs tremble before he's even touched her. Grazing the insides of her thighs with his teeth, he smiles to himself as she wriggles her hips, lifting her ass from the bed so she can thrust her aching pussy toward him. He craves the taste of her more than anything,

"Étienne, please."

Goddamn, he's drunk on her. She's so beautiful, so perfect. He'll give her everything she wants. His palm skates down the inside of her thighs, the silken softness of her skin just as intoxicating as the way she wriggles down the bed toward him.

No more teasing, it's agony for them both. She bucks her hips against him as he licks her, her breath heavy and broken by moans and gasps. His tongue traces her folds, exploring each divine inch of her.

He works slowly, kissing the firm swell of her clit with his lips and tongue, drawing back the hood beneath her curls so he can kiss her deeper like she does when she's on top. She sucks in a breath, tangling her fingers in his hair.

Having her on his face was incredible, his entire purpose on earth distilled into that one act; to pleasure her. But this…this is perfection. Watching her writhe against the pillows, her fingers grasping at him, twisting into the bedsheets, her cheeks and tits flushed pink as he licks her. Every gasp, every moment of pleasure she feels is because of him. Just to think about it makes his cock pulse, and he can't help but grind his hips against the mattress.

Her eyes screw tight as he licks her harder, edging her toward her climax. She moans his name, the sound of it sending lightning bolts crackling down his spine as her body tenses and her breath grows heavy. She comes, gasping, her hips thrusting up off the mattress, her pussy hot and wet and throbbing against his lips.

And when she crumples back down to earth, one arm draped over her forehead and the other beckoning for him to join her on the pillows, he kisses his way back up her body, cherishing every inch of her.

"Holy shit," she whispers.

"I love you."

Fuck. He freezes. His mind races in full panic mode, reaching for some way to take it back. He means it. God, he means it with his whole fucking heart, but it's too soon. Far too soon. She's going to push him away, build that defense back up to protect herself from him.

The slow caress of her palm on his cheek stills his panicked thoughts. "What?"

"I'm sorry." He's breathless, caught somewhere between terror and arousal. "It slipped out."

"Did you mean it? If you were just caught up on the moment you can take it back, but… did you actually mean it?"

His eyes meet hers, and the warmth in her gaze melts some of his fear. He nods.

Her lips curve into a smile which sends flutters through his belly. "Étienne, I love you too."

Those words flip a switch in both of them. They collide, hungry for one another, two people who have deprived themselves for so long, finally feasting on what they needed most. He loves her, recklessly, completely.

He's lightheaded with desire as she tells him to get up onto his knees and rolls a condom onto his cock. She settles back on the pillows, knees parted, her ankles gently nudging his ass as she readies herself to wrap her legs around him.

He enters her slowly, relishing the shiver of pleasure rolling though his body. She lifts her head from the pillow, kissing his shoulders and chest as he thrusts into her, slowly, savoring, tormenting them both. Her body is hot and wanting, her pussy wet and tight around his cock.

She digs her nails into his back as she moans, and the

mixture of pleasure and pain is almost too much to bear. He needs more. He has to fuck her hard and fast.

***

Something switches inside him. She sees it in his eyes, a fierce, primal urge, and he can't hold back any longer. Liz was right. Without the tethers holding him down he fucks like a jackhammer, short, sharp thrusts sending wave after wave of pleasure through her body.

He raises onto his knees, lifting her legs over his shoulders so he can thrust deeper. His fingers grip her hips almost painfully, but everything about it is perfect. He is perfect. The weight of him on top of her is as sexy as it is comforting. She feels safe and loved, and oh so much pleasure.

And she is. She is loved. And so is he.

She trails her hands over his body and rubs her fingers over the taught buds of his nipples, coaxing a deep, savage growl from him.

"I want you to come again," he gasps, his breath hard and fast.

"I'll need help."

"Tell me what to do."

He stops thrusting while she reaches over to her bedside drawers and pulls out a small, curved, neon pink vibrator. When she puts it on her clit and flicks on the switch, his lip curls into a snarl as he drops her legs and dips his head to suck one of her nipples.

Jordan's eyes close tight as she loses herself to the sensation. The vibrator, pinned between their bodies, rubbing and humming against her clit, the relentless thrust of his cock in her pussy, his tongue and lips against her nipple. Her second orgasm builds quickly, tightening like a spring, until she cries out and pleasure breaks over her, ripping through every sinew of her body.

"God, yes. Fuck." Étienne's back bows as he thrusts deep into her once more, his body shuddering as he comes and he can no longer support his weight with his arms.

She holds him as he collapses onto her, his head between her tits, his cock still inside her and his long, dark eyelashes fluttering against his cheeks.

He shifts his hips just enough for her to retrieve the vibrator and switch it off before discarding it on the bed.

Breathing in the scent of his hair, she kisses the top of his head and brushes his back with soothing caresses. "Thank you."

His eyes flutter open, and he shifts his weight back onto his forearms. "Jordan," he whispers, his gaze lovingly tracing her features. A soft sigh escapes him. "I mean it. I really do."

"I do too." She brings up a hand to his cheek, her heart swelling as he leans into her touch.

How anyone so beautiful could exist in this world she doesn't know. But he does. He's here. He's real. And he's hers.

***

"Thank you," he says as they eat barbeque chicken pizza, sitting beside each other on the black leather couch.

Jordan bites into the sourdough crust, relishing the crisp, perfectly baked dough. Pizza is always her favorite, but good pizza after amazing sex is next level. "For?"

"Everything." He takes another bite and chews slowly before swallowing. "I know this can't have been easy."

"It kind of was," she smiles, taking another slice. "I was a little nervous, but I know I can trust you. You're the first man I've had in my home who wasn't directly related to me, other than Finn, obviously."

Étienne grins at the mention of the drummer. "He's going to be so smug when he finds out we're together."

"He already knows," Jordan chuckles, wiping her fingers on a napkin. "They all do. Apparently, we weren't exactly subtle."

"Oh. Does it bother you?"

"No," she says without hesitation. "Not at all."

In fact, the only regret she has is that she didn't plan the evening better. When Étienne leaves, she picks at the remnants of the cold pizza, her lips still tingling from the bristles of his beard, and wishes she'd asked him to stay. Without him, her house is quiet and a little too empty, exactly the way she had liked it before. But now it isn't enough.

She smiles as she sits on the couch and traces her fingers over her lips. She misses him, his conversation, his kisses, his far-too-irresistible face, the way his nose crinkles when he's really, truly smiling.

A light in the corner of her eye makes her heart leap, her phone almost vibrating off the arm of the couch. In the second it takes for her to reach out and take it the hope that Étienne is calling makes her pulse race. She calms almost instantly as Mia's name glows blue on the screen.

"Hey?" she answers.

There's a short silence before Mia's voice sounds. "Are you alone?"

"Yes?"

Another pause. "You suuuure?"

Jordan laughs, rolling her eyes at Mia's playful tone. "I'm suuuure."

"Good. When did he leave?"

There's little use in denying it. The rest of the Vixens know, no doubt thanks in part to Finn, and also maybe a little due to hers and Étienne's subtle-as-a-brick flirting. "Ten, fifteen minutes ago… why?"

"Ah," Mia sighs. "Finn just posted *Bloodlust* on the forum. It's still a little rough but we figured we'd give the die-hards early access. I thought it'd be a fun couples' activity for the two of you to listen to it."

Jordan is already pulling out her laptop as she scowls and shakes her head, fighting back a smile. "You're terrible."

"This coming from the woman keeping the prime cuts of gossip from her friends. You could've told me, you know."

"I know. If it was any other guy, I would've, but he's a Vixen, and you know I swore off ever dating a band member after—" she clamps her lips shut. She won't even say his name anymore, won't waste another breath acknowledging his existence. "I didn't even want to admit it to myself."

She puts in the password to her laptop and gives it a moment to load before typing the forum's URL.

"I'm happy for you, Jordo. I really am. I have to call the others and let them know about the song, but I'll talk to you tomorrow, okay?"

"Yeah, see you."

Jordan sighs as the call ends and the band's forum page opens. She tries not to cringe as the banner loads and she's confronted with the image of her twenty-three-year-old self, blue haired, pouting and sporting a black and silver studded belt and neon pink wrist-warmers.

"Mortifying."

Sure enough, there's a post from Finn pinned to the top of the page:

Hey there, you gorgeous lot, we thought you might like a sneak peek at what we've been working on. Here's your chance to see if Étienne's voice is as pretty as his face. This is a little song we call Bloodlust Beautiful. Peace, Finn.

P.S. I'm still the token hot guy, okay? Don't think I don't read your comments.

P.P.S. Oh yeah, we're performing this song (among others) at Ghoulfest next week. Get ready to sing your fucking hearts out. Links to tickets are above.

Love you.

Jordan chuckles and shakes her head. She scrolls down to the images of the band in the recording studio until she finds one of Étienne. His eyes are screwed tight, his chest full and broad as he sings. The sight of him turns her lungs to stone and sends tingles shooting though her body. She can still feel him on every inch of her skin, but it isn't enough.

Beneath the images is a link to a video. Holding her breath, she clicks and waits for the song to load. The name Vixen's Wail blazes red in the center of the black screen as the music begins. Liz's keyboard breaks the silence and soon after is accompanied by Nic's violin. One by one the instruments come in, until her cello moans deep and low beneath it all and she can breathe again. It sounds far better on the track than it did to her perfectionist's ear. The wonders of mixing.

Mia begins to sing, and the band sounds incredible, as

always. Jordan adored their first album, but she can already tell this one is going to be even better. They've matured, improved, taken on criticism and feedback, lived life more fully.

She closes her eyes and lets the song wash over her, raising the hairs on her arms and the back of her neck. And then Étienne's verse starts.

He's just as beautiful as she knew he would be. The song allows him to loosen the reins on his impressive vocal range, sending shivers through her body. His gasps and moans are accentuated on the track and make it even harder for her to breathe.

God, the sounds he makes when he's inside her, in those moments when his entire universe begins and ends with her. He rocks her whole fucking world, and she knows she rocks his. She fights back a smile as she squeezes her thighs together. She's still wet from his touch, still tingling from the memories of his lips on her pussy, from the feral rhythm of his thrusts.

Slipping her hand beneath the waistband of her leggings, she minimizes the video window and scrolls to find the image of him singing as she circles her clit with her fingertip. She's tender, sensitive, her clit already swollen with need. It has been a long time since she felt this insatiable.

Her breath breaks as she scrolls through images of him. His head is thrown back, his eyes screwed tight and neck straining as he sings, an expression startlingly similar to the face he makes when he comes.

The pressure builds in her core as she strokes herself harder and faster, imagining him on top of her, thrusting into her while he buries his face in her tits, sucking her nipples, biting her, claiming her. She comes hard as the song reaches its crescendo and Étienne delivers a final soul-affirming note which drowns out her own broken moans.

She sits slumped on the couch, breathless and shuddering as the song fades, and she's left with nothing but the hammering of her heart.

Her phone lights up with a text from Mia:

Did you listen yet? Do you like it?

Jordan chuckles as she sits upright and replies: *Fucking awesome.*

She's about to log out of the forum when a little red balloon pops up in the top right-hand corner of the laptop screen. It's a notification, telling her she has a private message. Her heart skips as she clicks it. So far, she's only ever had DMs from Étienne and she grins at the prospect of telling him she just came while listening to his voice.

But her heart plummets as the message pops up on the screen.

DannyShreds: I bet he doesn't fuck you like I used to fuck you, baby girl.

SEVENTEEN

The heat coursing beneath the surface of Étienne's skin is no longer lust. It's fear. He throws his jacket on the arm of his couch and sits on the floor, pressing his fingertips to his eyelids as he breathes deep, unsatisfying breaths.

He knows the band's fans are listening to him right now, judging whether he fits into their world. As soon as Finn called to tell him about the upload, his confidence plummeted, and he became absolutely sure that he's a fraud and always has been.

He picks up his phone and considers calling Jordan to have her talk him through it, but a knock on the door sends his pulse skyrocketing.

Pulling himself to his feet, he heads to the door. Hope swells in his chest. It could be her, finding that being away apart is just as awful for her as it is for him.

But his smile fades as he opens the door. The man standing there is tall and sullen, with long black hair and a long black goatee in the center of his chin.

Great.

For years Dan and Étienne played together, entertaining the crowds at weddings and birthdays. Étienne would sing, and Dan would play guitar. A great musician, but a pain in the ass to deal with.

The guitarist rakes his gaze over Étienne and smirks. "I've been trying to get through to you."

Étienne sighs. "Oh, you have? My phone has been acting up."

"Sure it has," Dan sighs and rolls his eyes. "You have a few things of mine. Headphones, cables, that kind of stuff. I'd like them back."

"Yeah sure, one sec." Étienne makes to close the door, but hesitates when he realizes he has only a vague idea of where the cables might be. Honestly, he can't even remember borrowing them. "You can come in, if you want to?"

"Thanks. I think we need to talk anyway." Dan strides into the apartment, his eyes scouring the family photos on the wall. The guitarist casts a derisive look at Étienne before he slumps onto the couch, legs splayed wide. "How are things going with Vixen's Wail? They got you dressing like Count Chocula yet?"

The goading tone of his voice raises Étienne's hackles, but he distracts himself by searching through a tub of equipment sitting in the corner of the living room. "I'm just recording a couple of tracks with them. Nothing permanent."

"Seriously?" Dan's eyes grow wide. "They're just letting you go?"

"I'm just a guest singer."

"Those assholes. They don't know what they're missing."

"They were doing just fine before me."

"I guess." The guitarist picks something from between his teeth and rolls it between his thumb and middle fingertip.

"So does that mean that if I had a gig lined up, you might be available?"

Étienne frowns. "You were the one who said we should split."

"I made a mistake, dude." Dan sits back, spreading his arms along the back of the couch, no doubt wiping his fingers back there. "You're the best fucking vocalist in this city. I need you back."

He'd be lying if he said his ego wasn't at least a little stroked and that the prospect of extra income wasn't tempting. "I'll think about it."

"Someone sent a request for a quote. It's a big wedding, lakeside vineyard, gazebos, all that shit. It'd be a decent chunk of change for you."

Étienne hates that he's even considering it. He wasn't as happy as a wedding singer, but the money was good… and necessary. His days with the Vixens are numbered, and he doesn't want to have to rely on Finn's charitable nature the next time his car breaks down, or even worse, ask Jordan and reveal to her what a failure he is. "Hell, why not. Just once, right?"

"Sure. You won't regret it."

Étienne's ears burn as he fights back the urge to bring up the shitty comments Dan made about his talent the last time they spoke. Instead, turns back to the box and resumes his search.

Desperate to get the guitarist out of his house, he puts his hands on a set of headphones, the nicest ones he owns, and holds them out. "I think these are yours."

Dan takes them without hesitation and smiles companionably. "Oh, thanks."

"Don't mention it."

The guitarist steps back wrapping the wire around the headset. "It's good to see you, you know. I heard you were doing well for yourself and I'm glad to see it. If a little jealous."

"Yeah," Étienne stands and searches for another box. "I did get your fucking asshole text."

A bark of laughter bursts from Dan. "Man, you know how it is. One minute you're riding high, fucking bridesmaids, mothers of the brides," he smirks. "Even a bride or two. Then suddenly your band has split and your singer is cozying up to some hot big-titty goth chick. I'll admit I was pissed."

"Right," Étienne bites back the urge to kick him out of his apartment. "Was there anything else you're missing?"

"No, I think this is fine," Dan turns and heads out toward the front door. When he opens it, he turns back to speak. "You know, if we go ahead with the vineyard gig, I'd like us to maybe work on some original songs together."

"Oh?"

"Yeah. Honestly, I don't think talent like yours should be wasted on covers of other people's songs. Hell, we could give Vixen's Wail a run for their money. Make them regret not signing you on permanently."

Étienne's chest burns with a breath he's all too aware he's holding. Fronting a band again, but singing original songs, building his own fanbase, playing on a real stage and selling out venues has been his dream since the first time he sang. Surely Jordan would want that for him too? "Maybe." There's a red taxi parked outside which he assumes is Dan's. "Your cab is waiting."

"Just consider it. That's all I ask."

The lure of extra money calls to him. If he could start

bringing in a steady wage again, he could treat Jordan the way he truly wants to and he wouldn't have to give up his dreams. The fact that Dan inflates his ego a little barely factors into it… well… almost barely. "I will."

Dan smiles and places his hands on Étienne's shoulders, staring into his eyes. "You're meant for more than just a backing singer on a couple of tracks in some shitty vampire band. Just remember that, okay?"

He nods as his stomach churns. "I'll be in contact."

"Yeah," Dan grins. "And maybe get your phone fixed so you don't miss out on any more opportunities."

The cab pulls away leaving Dan behind, but Étienne closes the door, unwilling to spend a moment longer with the jerk. He can order his own damn taxi.

Heading back inside, Étienne finally draws breath comfortably. Dan might be a dick, but he's the best shot Étienne has at making music his career. Perhaps this time it'll be different.

A paycheck's a paycheck.

He slumps onto the floor in the living room and pulls out his laptop, waiting for it to load so he can listen to the Vixen's Wail track, and lamenting the loss of his best headphones.

"Asshole."

He isn't sure if he's talking to Dan or himself.

***

Jordan freezes, panic tearing through her body, torn between the urge to escape, and the instinct to stay perfectly still and go unnoticed.

"Are you getting out?" the cab driver calls over his shoulder.

It can't be real. It can't be. It has to be some trick of the dark, her vision blurring in the glow of the streetlights and obscuring the world.

And yet, no matter how hard she tries to deny it, Étienne, the man she loves, is standing on the doorstep, laughing and talking to the man who once tried to ruin her life.

How could a world which only minutes ago was so perfect suddenly turn to hell?

When she saw the message from Danny she'd panicked. Without her car she felt even more helpless. She'd called a cab and paced back and forth in her living room until it arrived. She needed to get out. She couldn't be alone.

But it wasn't Finn she needed. In that moment when she felt her most vulnerable, she just wanted to be with Étienne.

She didn't expect him to stand between her and Danny, menacing and seething like Finn once had. In fact, she hadn't expected him to see Danny at all. She wanted comfort. Safety. Him.

But staring out of the taxi window, her pulse lancing through every part of her body, she knows there and then that she was wrong. She was wrong about so much.

The driver clears his throat. "Excuse me, miss?"

"Sorry." Her voice is barely a whisper. She turns to the driver and speaks to the back of his head. "Sorry I need to go somewhere else."

"No problem. Where to?"

Mia lives the furthest away.

She gives the cab driver the address and sits back, staring straight ahead. Not a single clear thought runs through her mind. Just fear and betrayal and confusion. They clamor for her attention, turning into an oppressive haze which drowns out the sound of the car's engine and the sight of the streets whirring past her window. By the time the cab pulls up outside Mia's home, Jordan can barely see straight.

As she knocks on the black wooden door, she finds herself struggling to remember if she even paid the driver, but he's no longer parked at the bottom of Mia's driveway. She must have.

"Jordan?" Mia's husband, August stands with the door wide, his eyes narrowed as he searches her face. "What are you doing here?"

And then it collapses onto her. The shock of seeing Étienne and Danny so friendly with each other, that the best thing in her life right now is just as tainted as everything else. Tears burn her eyes.

"God, I'm sorry I should've called first." Her lip quakes as she speaks.

"You're fine. We were just watching a movie. What's up?"

"Is Mia home?"

August nods and ushers her inside, checking over her shoulder as if something is behind her. Heart racing, she turns to check too, but the driveway is empty.

While Mia's house looks like any other nice suburban home on the outside, the inside is like being teleported to some sumptuous gothic kingdom. The hallway has matte black walls, decorated with exquisitely framed Vixen's Wail posters. Slipping off her shoes, Jordan's feet sink into the thick, pristine white carpet.

She follows August into the living room, to where Mia reclines on a black velvet couch, surrounded by plush wine-red pillows. The sight of the band's vocalist, dressed in black velour sweat pants and a matching cropped sweater catches Jordan off guard. In almost a decade of playing with the Vixens, she has only seen Mia out of her on-stage attire a handful of times.

"Baby, are you okay?" Mia asks August, sitting upright and setting a bowl of popcorn aside. "What's wrong."

Her husband steps aside to give Jordan the floor.

"I'm so sorry, I should have called ahead. I just didn't know where else to go." Jordan's eyes scan the room, taking in the sumptuous, meticulously kept décor. Every time she comes to Mia's home, she feels unkempt and out of place. "Étienne…"

Mia sits forward, her features hardening. "What did he do?"

"I don't know." The simple truth falls from her lips. She doesn't know. If she had a year to work it out, she couldn't even guess what conceivable reason Étienne would have for inviting Danny to his home. Jordan opened up to him about her shitty ex, but she had never once mentioned his name or how to find him. Perhaps Danny was the one who went looking for him. Whatever happened, they looked so amiable with each other. It doesn't make sense. The Étienne she knows and loves wouldn't do this. Not if he truly loved her. Would he?

Does she know him at all?

"I don't know," she says again.

Mia is just as confused as she is, as she tells her what happened, both the message on the forum, and that Étienne and Danny were together and friendly. They sit alone together in the living room, August excusing himself and retreating to his study upstairs.

"Shit." Jordan rubs her hands over her face, completely

forgetting her eye makeup. It doesn't matter. She's sure she looks like a blotchy, puffy mess anyway. "This is why I never wanted to get involved with another band member."

"There has to be some explanation," Mia sighs, tapping her long, pointed black fingernails together. "I had reservations about him, but he never struck me as malicious."

"Me neither. But maybe that's just it. Maybe he just pretends to be sweet and caring to get his own way. To get me into bed…" Hot shame scalds her, rolling beneath the surface of her skin.

"Hey," Mia says. Her tone is firm but kind. "Don't even for one moment think you did anything wrong by sleeping with him. Okay? You're a grown-ass adult and so is he."

"You're right." Jordan sighs and sits a little more upright.

"But this just doesn't sound right to me. If you never told him Danny's name, how would he even find him?"

"No, Danny must have found him. I know he's active on the forums. He would have seen Étienne's name on there and with a name like that he's easy to track down. Unless they knew each other all along." She exhales shakily. "Mia, what if he's given him my address?"

"Then the Vixens will have their first group murder project." Mia reclines on the couch, tapping the end of one of her braids against the sharp arc of her cheekbone.

The pain of Étienne's betrayal weighs heavy in Jordan's chest, turning her lungs to rigid steel. "Mia, I…" She works her tongue around her arid mouth. "I told him I loved him."

The vocalist exhales heavily, raising her face to the ceiling. "Shit."

"I know."

"And do you love him?"

Jordan's throat clenches. Her tongue presses firm against

the top of her mouth as nausea rolls through her stomach. She does love him, but she shouldn't. She trusted him and it was a mistake. One she won't rush to ever make again.

"No." She shakes her head, trying more than anything to convince herself. "I just got caught up in the moment. But I can't love someone if I can't trust them, can I?"

Mia nods and breathes a sigh of relief. "Okay. Well, that's one less thing to worry about. You can stay here tonight if you want?"

"Thank you."

"And we can talk to Finn about him driving you to and from practice and recording. Whatever helps you feel safe."

At last Jordan's breath flows freely. With every inhale her shoulders fall by a hair's breadth. "I don't know what I'd do without you."

"We're Vixens," Mia shrugs, picking a piece of popcorn from her bowl and holding it between her talons. "We have each other's backs, always."

F or the first time since their first kiss, an entire day passes where he doesn't hear from Jordan. He checks his phone repeatedly, finding nothing but friend requests from fans, and a text from Dan:

Dude. I'm so excited for what's to come. This is going to be awesome. I can

feel it.

But Étienne doesn't feel awesome.

He tries to tell himself that Jordan is just playing it cool, taking some time to think things over after the intensity of their last night together. She told him she loves him, and he tries to hold onto that as another day passes without any contact.

By the third day he's truly worried. His mind begins to race, telling him she's had second thoughts, or that she's hurt and needs him while he's just sitting on his couch chatting to fans on the forums. He calls her phone, but it goes to voice-mail instantly. His hands shake as he calls Finn.

"Yeah?" The drummer's voice is unusually curt. "What's up?"

Étienne's chest tightens a little. Jordan said everyone in the band knew about them, but what if it isn't something he can just openly talk about? "Hey man, I was just calling to make sure everything's okay."

In the heavy silence which answers, Étienne all too aware of the sound of his own breathing. The heavy thud of a door closing sounds on the other end of the phone, followed by the steady roar of distant traffic. "Sorry," Finn's voice returns. "I just needed to step outside."

"Oh!" Étienne sighs with relief. "You're at the recording studio, aren't you?"

"Yeah, just working on those other tracks."

He's so foolish. It all seems so obvious now. Jordan hasn't contacted him because she's in the recording studio, unable to use her phone, and probably exhausted by the end of the day.

"Cool."

"Look," Finn says. "Whatever is going on with you and Jordan, you need to stop it, okay? I don't want to have to deal with another of her ex-boyfriends, so I'd appreciate it if you just backed off."

The world comes to a screeching halt. Étienne's throat

dries out as Finn's words play through his head over and over. "Ex? What?"

"We're still prepared to work with you for the festival, but after that we've taken the decision to look elsewhere for guest vocalists on future tracks."

Étienne can't speak. His mouth forms the shapes of syllables, but no sound comes. Thoughts clutter his head as his heart pounds.

"I'll send your royalty checks in the mail." Finn's tone is one of finality. He's all business. "I'm sorry, Étienne. I have to look out for the Vixens."

The call ends. Étienne stares at his phone as the screen goes dark. His reflection stares open-mouthed at him. Something has happened. Something bad.

He tries to think back to when he left Jordan's house. They kissed on the doorstep, and he left her reluctantly, casting a longing glance back at her as she watched him go. He thought she'd wanted him to stay just as badly as he wanted to. Was he wrong to leave? Was he wrong to even assume she felt the same?

He glances up at the pictures on the wall. His Mémé and Granddaddy hand in hand, laughing together at some joke he wasn't even alive to hear, captured in a moment of love he's beginning to think he'll never get to experience for himself.

"What the fuck is happening?"

He spends the next few days wondering, replaying every moment in his head, searching for some clue as to how it all could have gone so wrong. As the week rolls by and he's no closer to an answer, the only person who answers his calls is Dan.

The guitarist answers after two rings, his low drawl even

more slurred than normal. "You better not be having second thoughts. I already told the vineyard couple we'd be there and took a deposit."

His words barely even register with Étienne as he picks at a tattered hole in the knee of his jeans. He'd like to say that the hole was part of their design, but that would be a lie. These past couple of days he hasn't taken any care at all over his appearance. "No, we're still on."

"Thank fuck."

"I just needed to hear a friendly voice."

A machine gun fire chuckle sounds on the other end of the call. "What's up?"

Étienne glances up at the ceiling. "I don't even know."

"Women trouble?"

"Yeah, I guess."

"Fuck 'em." Dan grunts on the other end. "Look, I didn't want to say anything, but that cello chick, Jordan. She's… well let's just say she has a reputation."

The world drops from beneath Étienne as he sits upright, ears burning. "What do you mean?"

"Her and… what's his name… the drummer?"

"Finn?"

"Yeah. From what I hear—and this is from a reliable source—they have something going on. Like a friends-with-benefits kind of deal. Only he's very possessive over her. Every time she gets close to a guy, he scares them off so he can have her for himself."

Étienne doesn't hear much more after that. Pieces begin falling into place. The longing looks she gave Finn at his wedding, the casual way she hugs him. It was Finn who told him it was over between the two of them. He hates it, hates that he's even thinking it, but there's no other explanation he can think of. The knowledge that he spent weeks fawning after someone who only ever saw him as a side piece boils his blood.

Not again. He's better than that, and he'll be damned if he spends another moment pining over Jordan. He won't be used.

"You still there?" Dan asks.

"Yeah." Étienne sucks in a breath and sits up straight. "Yeah, I'm good. So, tell me about this vineyard gig again. What kind of deposit are we talking?"

EIGHTEEN

Jordan pulls in a breath as Finn's van stops on the gravel of the festival's backstage parking lot. Étienne's car isn't there yet and his absence loosens a knot in her chest.

Outwardly, she's incredible; fresh black-to-blue ombre hair, long, flowing black skirt and a low-cut black lace top which shows off her rack to its full magnificent potential.

But inside, she's a mess.

Wide green fields surround them on all sides, apart from one which is covered in a dense forest of yellow corn stalks. The enormous scaffold of the festival stage peers over the top of the stalks in the distance, and even though the sun is still high and bright, various stage lights are already lit and turning on their rig as the organizers work out the technical aspects of the show.

"Alright. Looks like we're clear," Finn mutters as he turns off his van's ignition and blows out a breath of his own. "Jesus this is fucking awkward."

"Yeah," Jordan sighs. "I'm sorry."

"You've got nothing to be sorry about."

"I know you liked him."

Finn turns to her and smiles before giving a bitter huff of laughter. "Not as much as I like you though."

Her heart warms a little, but it still presses painful and hard against her ribs. "I was starting to think he could be The One, you know? I kept telling myself I was falling too hard and too fast, but I couldn't slow down."

"You don't ever have to explain myself to me," Finn says. "Yeah, I liked Étienne, but I'm on your side no matter what. I'm more than happy to tell every guy in the world to fuck off until we find the one who is good enough to deserve you."

Jordan leans across the space between their seats to hug him, and the moment his arms are around her she has to fight back tears.

"You can cry if you want to," he says. "I don't mind if you snot on me."

"No," she pulls back. "My makeup took forever. Fuck that." She shakes out her arms and presses the sides of her fingers below her eyes, making sure her mascara hasn't smudged. "Let's just go out there, run through the rehearsal, and get the fuck out of here."

"Sounds like a plan." Finn grins as he opens the door on his side and jumps out.

As his door slams shut, Jordan sits in the silence, slowly, rhythmically breathing in the cool late October air. She had imagined being at this festival so many times, imagined watching Étienne on stage, performing as the frontman he was born to be. But now she doesn't know if she can even look at him.

It has been a week, and she's still no closer to figuring out what he and Danny had been doing together. Finn took great pleasure in blocking DannyShreds from the forum and posting a pinned notice at the top of the chat about their zero-tolerance policy toward harassing band members.

Danny hasn't come to her house and he hasn't messaged again. The irrational notion that she had somehow imagined the whole thing frequently infiltrated her thoughts.

The clunk of her door opening makes her jump.

"You coming?" Finn asks, standing at her side.

"Yeah." She climbs down out of her seat and brushes herself off. The sweet smell of vegetation floods the air as she takes another calming breath. Whatever happens today she'll see Étienne, and she'll remain calm.

The distant sound of a band on the stage sets her heart racing. No matter what, this is huge for the Vixens. She won't lose sight of that. Even though the man who she suspected was the love of her life has betrayed her in a way she never thought possible.

Finn whistles the melody to *Cacoffiny*, one of his favorite songs of theirs, as he slides open the side door of the van and begins to unload his kit. He hands Jordan her cello case and a cymbal to carry, before stacking his big bass drum and a few smaller ones in a pile for him to lug in one go.

"Hey," he says, as he slides the van's door shut with his heel. "Let's not let asshole guys overshadow the fact that we're headlining a goddamn festival."

He's right, she knows he's right. But even as he speaks, Étienne's little blue hatchback heads toward them. She'd recognize it anywhere. It's blue like his eyes.

Her gut tightens as Étienne parks the car on the other

side of the lot, and the air around her is no longer cool and crisp. The stifling stench of rotting vegetation churns her stomach. Seconds roll by but Étienne doesn't get out.

"Come on," Finn grunts, hitching up the drums so he has a better grip on them. "Let's just rock this fucking shit."

Jordan nods and walks close to Finn, fighting the urge to check over her shoulder all the while.

É tienne expected he'd see them together, but not right away. He doesn't even recognize Jordan at first. Her hair is no longer bubblegum pink, but black, fading to blue at the tips. Even from this distance he can tell she's stunning, her flowing skirt and tight top showing off her figure. She looks like a queen, and she has decided he isn't worthy of her.

Finn stands by her side, huge and intimidating.

Étienne is almost tempted to turn around and leave, but that would be letting them win. The rest of the band shouldn't suffer just because of them.

Étienne Moore does not give up. He's a born frontman and he won't pass up his chance to sing on that stage. Hell, even if Finn and Jordan are laughing behind his back, he'll put his heart into every goddamn note. Mia wanted passion from him, and the hurt he's felt these past few days is more than enough to power him through.

With all the pain in his heart he could scream the world to rubble.

But as he watches them head off toward the stage, the anger simmering though his body dissipates, leaving nothing but an empty, charred blackness.

Numb, he waits a few minutes after Jordan and Finn are out of sight before he gets out of the car and makes his way across the parking lot. Gravel crunches beneath his feet as the breeze rustles the cornstalks. He follows the sound of the band already on stage, their haunting melody both a siren's call and a warning.

He gives his name at the desk to collect his artist's pass, holding his breath as he fully expects to have been left off the list. One last humiliation, one last kick of the boot. But he's there, and his name is spelled correctly. He's in.

This should be one of the best days of his life, but as he threads the lanyard through his belt loop and makes his way backstage, none of it feels the way it should.

An enormous, bearded roadie barges past, lugging an massive black case in his tattooed arms. He casts a scathing look over Étienne, before noting the pass on his hip and walking away.

There are around twenty backstage staff rushing around, shouting commands and cusses at each other, reading off lists and clipboards. All of them are dressed in black shirts with the words "Ghoulfest event staff" printed in pumpkin orange.

Étienne isn't sure where he's supposed to be, but he's fairly certain he's in everyone's way. He makes his way to the other end of the stage, to where it's quieter and he can put his thoughts in order.

"Étienne! Here."

The sound of Mia calling his name from a row of trailers behind the stage stirs a spark of hope among cold ashes, a longing for a familiar face. He should be celebrating making it this far and headlining a festival, but as he makes his way toward a silver trailer with "Vixens's Wail" incorrectly spelled on the sign on the door, it's as though he's walking through a noxious haze.

Before he steps inside, he balls his fists, and reminds himself he's just there to perform. He can do this. He's performed for bickering families, furious couples. He's used to singing through difficult situations. This is no different. Dragging in a breath, he steps over the threshold.

Immediately his stomach flutters. Jordan sits at a dressing table, wrapping her hair around a curling iron, her smokey eyes downcast. He was right, she is stunning, and in that moment, he despises every atom of his body, because every one of them still yearns for her.

He nods in place of a greeting, shoving his hands in his pockets as he tries to control his breathing. Mia and Finn are stood close to the door, arms folded over their chests. Liz is sat by a window, peering beneath the blinds, clearly looking for someone. Nic, Anya and Tamika huddle in the corner, looking at him as though they were only just whispering about him. The disdain in Finn's eyes he expected, but every member of the band looks at him as though he's dirt. All but one.

Jordan can't even look at him, and he realizes she doesn't just hold disdain for him. She *despises* him.

"You ready?" Mia says abruptly. She's wearing yellow feline contact lenses, and the way her eyes pass over him, otherworldly and detached, send a shiver through his body.

But it's nothing compared to the chill he gets from Jordan's eyes as she finally raises them long enough to look at him in the reflection of the mirror. It only lasts a moment before she turns away again.

How can he sing like this? Every note he's ever sung with Vixen's Wail was for her, telling her how much he loves her, how incredible she is. But he can't do that anymore. Cold fear consumes his body as the band stands and prepares to head back to the stage.

He isn't ready.

Not by a long fucking shot.

Nineteen

She can't look at Étienne. She can't look because even just knowing he's in the same trailer as her makes her stomach flip. The familiar scent of him tightens her chest, and every muscle in her body tenses, begging her to go to him.

"You okay?" Mia whispers as the band begins to file out of the trailer.

Jordan doesn't answer until Étienne is out and down the steps. "Not really."

The vocalist puts her arms around her and pulls her into a crushing hug. "Just get through this and you never have to see him again. Okay?"

That hurts far more than it has any right to.

The band are unusually quiet as they climb the steps at the back of the stage and check in with an enormous, bearded roadie.

Jordan finds herself standing beside Liz, whose breath audibly catches as she gazes up at the stagehand.

"Let us know if anything is missing," the roadie grumbles

without so much as looking at the keyboardist. "You've got nearly twice as many instruments as any other band we have playing so something's bound to go wrong."

"Thank you," Liz says. She glances down at the roadie's thick, heavily tattooed forearms and bites her lip.

Under any other circumstances Jordan would be loving every moment of watching her friend so blatantly flirt, but being so close to Étienne, unable to touch him, unable to even look at him, saps all the joy and enjoyment from what should be an incredible day.

"You're up," the roadie tells them, and points them out onto the stage.

They head out as more roadies guide them to the spots where they'll stand. Jordan is off to the side with Nic as usual, and Mia is front and center behind her mic stand. Finn's excitement is anything but muted as he begins to thrash his drum kit, elevated on his own little stage.

As chaos reigns behind her, Jordan steps away from her mark and heads toward the very front of the stage, looking out over the vast field in front of them. The field where the audience will stand is surrounded by an enormous corn maze. Tomorrow their fans will have to make their way through the haunted maze to get to the stage. Ghoulfest was one of her favorite things to do as a teen, and now she's performing at it.

It doesn't feel as good as she thought it would.

The sun isn't far from setting and the overhead lighting casts them in an eerie blue glow. Somewhere off to the side, a smoke machine begins to whir, covering the floor with ethereal haze.

She's aware of Étienne before she sees him, a prickling warmth at her back which she isn't sure is a comfort or a warning. Glancing over her shoulder, the sight of him makes her heart squeeze. He stands at his mic, gazing out just as she was. The sadness in his eyes almost enough to bring her to her knees.

Part of her wants to confront him, to ask just what the fuck he thought he was doing with Danny. No matter how her thoughts twist and turn themselves in knots, she can't think of a single reason they would be talking to each other.

She's angry and hurt and afraid, and having him so close makes the lump in her throat swell painfully. Because more than anything, more than answers and a vent for her frustration, she wants him. She *craves* him.

"Jordan…" He says her name as though it physically hurts him to do so. No sooner does it leave his lips than he looks away, his throat flexing as he swallows. God how she wants to graze his throat with her teeth, to feel him writhe and groan beneath her. She hates that she wants it.

"Don't talk to me," she says, the bitter harshness in her voice alien to her. She storms past him, her long flowing skirt swirling the dry ice around her. She takes her seat on the stage and lifts her black electric cello off of its stand. "Let's just get through tonight and tomorrow, and then go our separate ways. As I said before, this has to be strictly professional." She tightens the screw on the end of her bow. "We should never have crossed that line."

That should be the end of it, but as he takes a step toward her, she knows he isn't done. "Just tell me why, Jordan. I just want to know—"

"You betrayed me," she spits, unable to hold onto it any longer. "I trusted you, and you betrayed me in the one way you knew would hurt me the most."

He stills, staring at her, his perfect lips parted as his cheeks turn pink. "I betrayed you?"

"Yes!" Fuck, she hates that he's so beautiful. She hates that she misses him and that she can't stop thinking about kissing him.

In her desperation she finds herself wondering what he would do if she stood up and pulled him to her, their lips colliding in a flurry of pain and pleasure. A swooping sensation low in her belly goads her, but as his cool eyes rake across her the spell ends. Thank God for the cello between her knees, holding her back from falling into his arms.

"And what about what you did to me?" He doesn't snarl or yell like Danny would have. His voice remains gentle and quiet, but his words hit her like a bullet to the heart. "I trusted you too. And you broke my heart, Jordan."

Even if she does want him, the cold indifference in those eyes tells her without doubt that he doesn't want her back. It's the sensation of having a bucket of ice water dumped over her. Every muscle in her body clenches as she freezes to the spot. "Me? What—?"

"Right!" the grumpy roadie bellows, breaking them apart. "Let's do a run through of…" He glances down at a clipboard, made flimsy in his large hands. "*Bloodlust Beautiful…* right, well that sounds delightful."

Étienne's words leave her astounded. Confused and wounded she focuses on something she does understand. Methodically checking the tuning on her cello, she tries not to look up at him as he walks back to his mic. Fuck him. There are billions of other men in the world, and she isn't about to spoil this opportunity over one of them.

"Alright," the roadie calls. "When you're ready."

Finn thrashes his sticks together four times, counting

them in, and the music starts. Right away goosebumps pebble Jordan's skin. The song sounded amazing on the recording, but up on the stage, amplified by the sound system, they sound…*huge.*

Despite her heartache, she can't help but feel a little elation as she plays. Every note Mia sings is perfectly crafted as she prowls around the stage, a vampire queen seeking her victim, hypnotic and mythical with her cat's eye contacts.

Mia's verse ends, and Jordan holds her breath, waiting for the heart-wrenching sound of Étienne's voice, his devastating response to the vampire's siren call.

But it doesn't come.

<hr>

Étienne has never known terror like it. Back in the rehearsal studio he was mortified that he froze up in front of the band, but this…

His throat is closed. Cold fear stiffens his spine. There are a hundred eyes on him. Not just the band, but the stage hands, the event staff, the organizers. All of them stare, their faces either pictures of pity, frustration or both. The band stop playing, the music petering out to a disjointed ruckus. He's let them down.

He's failed them yet again. And worse than that, somehow, somehow, he has betrayed Jordan.

His feet move out from under him before he even realizes what's happening. He bolts from the stage, tearing down the steps and through the gate. Corn stalks blur past him as he runs, his breath rushing from him in great gusts. He doesn't hear the band call out to him, and when he reaches his car, he turns to the empty parking lot and realizes they didn't follow him either.

"Fuck," he gasps, swiping a hand through his hair, his fingers latching onto a handful. He paces back and forth, desperate, breathless, lost. Alone.

TWENTY

Jordan's chest is hollow. Her heart is empty.

"You have got to be fucking kidding me!" Mia sighs as she throws her head back.

Tense doesn't cover it. The band gather in the center of the stage, panicked, afraid for their future while the roadie badgers them for their backup plan.

"We don't *have* a backup plan," Finn yells. "We didn't think this would happen."

The roadie curses and rubs his forehead. "Well, you need one now. Think fast."

Jordan sits behind her cello, waiting for them to turn to her and demand answers. Not that she could give them. She's spent a week trying to figure out what's happening.

The late October air is biting, but the heat coursing through her body is enough to stave it off.

"Maybe Finn could sing Étienne's part?" Liz offers.

"Finn sings like a goose in a woodchipper," Mia says before turning to Finn and adding, "No offense."

The drummer shrugs a shoulder from behind his kit. "No, that's fair."

Minutes feel like hours as they go back and forth, debating the best course of action out of a meagre handful of utterly shit options. There's so much pain and panic in their eyes, jaws clenched, hands grasping hair. Jordan's chest aches as she holds on to her breath. She has to do something.

She stands, legs shaking as she sets her cello back on the stand and joins the rest of the group.

"Do you know what's going on?" Liz asks as she approaches. "I thought he was cured of his stage fright. He hasn't done it in weeks."

He was. He told her that night at her house that he got over it by singing every word to her. The realization hits her like a fist. Perhaps, if he can't sing to her, he can't sing at all. "I think I need to talk to him."

"Are you sure?" Mia says. "If you're not okay with it we'll figure something out. I'll just sing both parts."

Jordan shakes her head. "I can do it. I'll find him."

"I'll drive," Finn adds. "We'll bring him back."

The big roadie clears his throat. "Uh, you still have to get through an actual song. We need to check the levels and finalize your setlist."

"Alright," Jordan says. "We'll run through the song and then go look for him. Mia, can you sing Étienne's part too?"

Mia nods and shrugs her slender shoulders. "We'll get it done."

It's a relief to have something of a plan. Jordan doesn't know what she'll say when finds Étienne, but if she has even the slightest hope of saving the show, she has to make peace between them, for the Vixens.

At least, that's what she tells herself. If she's honest, she wants answers. She wants to know what he said to Danny, and what he believes she did to break his heart.

As she takes her place on the stage and the band runs through the song, she listens to the lyrics. Lyrics he once sang to her, full of passion and a love which can withstand the ages. She closes her eyes and pictures herself standing in front of him, playing to the sorrow and pain in his eyes—agony he claims she put there.

None of it makes any sense, and she's done trying to unravel it. The Étienne she knows wouldn't betray her, and she knows for damn sure she did nothing but love him. But his heart is broken, and she needs to know why.

For better or for worse, it ends tonight.

As soon as the roadie tells them they're done, Jordan and Finn take off. They speed walk in silence through the corn stalks toward Finn's van. As expected, Étienne's car is long gone.

"Any idea where he went?" Finn asks as he unlocks the door.

Jordan jumps up into the passenger seat. "His apartment maybe? Try there first."

But he isn't there. When they pull up outside his home, the lights are off and his car isn't parked out front. Jordan's heart canters in her chest as panic starts to claw at her.

"Fuck."

"We'll find him," Finn assures her. He turns off the ignition and checks his phone while they're parked. "Let's just talk this through though first, okay."

"I don't know, Finn. He could be anywhere."

"No, I mean, let's talk the whole thing through. What happened that night? The night where you saw him with Danny."

Her chest empties as she thinks back to it. Despite every-thing, the memory of him, the way his body felt, the echo of the pleasure he gave her, still makes her heart squeeze. "I invited him to my house. He'd never been there before so it was a big deal. He knew it was. He told me he loved me, and I said it back. We shared a pizza and then he went home."

"And then you got the message from Danny, and when you went to Étienne's house Danny was there."

"Right."

Finn nods slowly. "And why do you think that is?"

She shrugs. "I don't know. Maybe now that Étienne knows my address, he was passing it onto Danny so he could find me again."

"But Danny hasn't been to your house. Since we banned him from the forum you haven't had any contact from him at all, have you?"

Shaking her head, she picks at a hangnail on the side of her thumb. "I've tried to make sense of it all week. One moment it was perfect, and the next... I just want to know *why*. What was he doing talking to Danny? If I don't find out I'll spend the rest of my life wondering, and..." She swallows hard as a lump starts to form in her throat. "I'm scared I won't ever trust anyone again."

Finn breathes a heavy sigh through his nose. "Look, I know I don't know Étienne as well as you do, but back when his car broke down, we talked." He glances at her, and even in the darkness she knows he's smiling a little. "We talked about you. We talked about how he felt, how he couldn't get you out of his head. I told him you've had trouble in the past, but I didn't say what or who. But he knew, and it hurt him just to think that anyone would ever hurt you." He shakes his head and looks out over the dashboard. "I just can't imagine that the same man I was talking to would betray you so bad. God, Jordan. I know he loved you."

Jordan laughs bitterly as a tear spills down her cheek. "He said he did…"

"No, he did. I know he did. He had that same look in his eyes when he talks about you that I had in all my wedding photos with Beth."

Those words cause Jordan to pull in a breath. Her heart aches as she remembers the way Étienne would look at her in those hazy, golden moments when she would let him wrap his arms around her.

It was real, and that's why it hurts so bad.

Finn grips the steering wheel with one hand and turns to face her again. "You said you love him…is that still true?"

It is, but she tries to suppress it, to hold on to it and bury it deep, deep down where no one can find it. But the harder she fights to cover it, the harder it pushes against her ribs, aching and growing. Like trying to kill a seed by entombing it in the dirt. The world blurs behind a veil of tears. "Yes. God, Finn, I love him so fucking much."

"Alright then." Finn nods and turns the ignition back on. "I almost missed out on the best thing in my life because I didn't communicate properly, so we're going to find him, and we're going to talk to him."

A strange mixture of hope and dread storm through her chest as she wipes her eyes carefully with the corner of her sleeve. "Okay, but we still have to find him."

Finn shakes his head. "Beth's texted me. I know where he is."

Once Étienne arrives at the factory, he doesn't know what to do. That burst of panic-sparked adrenaline fades, and he simply stands in the rehearsal room, breathless and embarrassed, clawing at ideas for his next move.

The key in his hand digs into his palm. Thank goodness Finn's wife, Beth was at the desk preparing to teach an art class and was willing to let him into the room.

Shit… Beth.

A voice inside his head tells him he should go back down and tell her everything Dan told him about Finn and Jordan.

But the thought of spreading his own pain is too much to bear right now. He needs a moment to gather his thoughts, and in the soundproof studio, he can think.

Jordan said he betrayed her in the one way he knew would hurt her the most. No matter how he twists it and turns it around in his mind, it just becomes more tangled.

He runs through that last night they spent together again when she invited him to her home. They'd had sex, they'd said they loved each other for the first time, and they'd eaten pizza. It was perfect, or so he'd thought.

He runs his hands through his hair. Somewhere in that perfect night he'd inadvertently betrayed her enough that she'd gone to Finn.

No, it doesn't fit.

That isn't Jordan. That isn't Finn.

Those aren't the people he knows. The people he loves.

The click of the door spikes his heart rate, and Finn's burly shape fills the doorframe. "Hey, can we talk?"

The drummer should be one of the last two people on this earth Étienne wants to speak to, but he can't help but feel a little comforted by his presence. "Yeah, come in… it's your rehearsal room anyway."

Finn steps inside and closes the door behind him. It's both a relief and a disappointment when Jordan doesn't come in with him. Perhaps she didn't feel he was worth chasing down.

Finn grunts a little as he sits on his drum stool and instinctively picks up a set of sticks. "So… what the fuck is going on?"

Étienne paces the room, threading his fingers through his hair. His heart thumps against his ribs. "I've been asking myself the same thing." He stops and turns to look at Finn. "I can't perform with the Vixens. I'm sorry. Keep the money, do whatever you have to do—"

"No." Finn states with a shake of his head. "No, you're performing on that stage if I have to drag you there and have that roadie tape your feet to the floor. You've worked too hard. We all have."

"I can't stand there with you and her, singing about love and knowing—"

"Knowing what?"

The air burns as Étienne tries to drag it down into his chest. "About you and Jordan. Knowing that you're together." As soon as the words leave his mouth, he regrets them.

Finn's eyebrows crease, his lips part in incredulity. "What —" The drummer laughs. "What the fuck?"

Étienne can't even respond. His cheeks burn as he looks away.

"Are you serious? That's what this is about?"

"No." Étienne says, his voice shaking. "No initially it wasn't about that. I only found out about that after days of not hearing from her. Everything was perfect, I had the job of my dreams, I had great friends who bought me donuts and fixed my fucking car, and I had this beautiful, incredible, talented woman who was somehow into me. And she said she loved me back. She didn't care that I'm not loaded or successful. She told me she loved me and then ghosted me." A hot tear rolls down his cheek, but he doesn't care. He can't be any more humiliated than he already is. "I don't know what's happening and the only person I could get to speak to me was my asshole ex-bandmate who told me the two of you were fucking each other and apparently I'm the only person in this city who doesn't know."

Finn's jaw twitches dangerously as he stands. "Do you really think that little of us? You were at my goddam wedding, dude. You said yourself, I fixed your car, I listened to you pour your heart out. Do you really think I'd betray you like that, not to mention my fucking wife? What the actual fuck, dude. Who do you think I am?"

Étienne opens his mouth to speak, but his retort is cut short by the sound of the door opening behind him.

"*How dare you.*"

He whirls around to face her. Her face is pale, her eyes dark with anger, but even then, his heart lifts at the sight of her. She's still in her stage clothes, black lace and flowing skirts. "Jordan…"

"I can't believe you think I would do that to you, or that Finn would do that to Beth."

He's plummeting, the earth falling out from beneath him. She must have been at the door, listening as he spoke to Finn. "I didn't know what to think."

"So, what?" Jordan spits. "You thought you'd track down my ex and… what? Tell me what you talked to him about."

"Your ex? I—"

"Wait." Finn steps between them, his voice sharp and sudden. "Just wait a second." He turns to Étienne, holding out a hand toward Jordan signaling for her to be still. "Before this gets any further, Étienne, what's the name of your ex-bandmate. Who told you Jordan and I were a thing? What's his name?"

Étienne pulls in a shaking breath as dismay and shame act as a tidal force deep inside him, churning his stomach. "Dan. His name is Dan."

The word is like a light switch. Just a simple flick which changes Finn's expression from anger to amusement.

For Jordan, it loosens something in her, allowing her to breathe for what must feel like an eternity. "You're serious? Danny? He's your ex-bandmate?"

Étienne nods, his mind bounding through possibilities. "Yeah. Why?"

Finn chuckles and raises his face to the ceiling, unleashing a loud and dramatic sigh. "Okay, you two have some talking to do. I'm going to go downstairs and interrupt my wife's class so I can kiss her because holy shit I need to. Neither one of you leaves this room until this is sorted, understand? Come down when you're done."

"Yes, Mom." Jordan sighs as she watches Finn go.

The moment of levity gives Étienne the opportunity to wipe his eyes and collect himself. Being alone with Jordan after everything that has passed should be terrifying or awkward. But to his surprise, it's comfortable, as though the world is slowly fitting back into place.

"Right," she sighs, walking over to the wall. Carefully, so as not to damage the soundproofing, she sits and leans back against it. Her skirts billow out around her, but she moves them over so there's space beside her for him. "I'll go first."

Twenty-One

She isn't sure how long they talk. It starts out as a simple explanation from both of them, growing into a conversation about how they both clearly need to work on trusting each other and communicating more openly.

When it's all laid out in front of them, the coincidence, the timing, the fated nature of it all, their exhaustion and elation takes over, and the conversation dissolves into laughter. And God, it's so good to laugh with him again, to see his nose crinkle, to feel something other than loss. To have clarity.

Her hand slips into his, finding its place, a bird coming home to roost where it knows it's safe and secure.

"Are the Vixens pissed at me?" he asks, his head pressed back against the wall.

"They're a little worried about what's going to happen tomorrow. Except Liz who just seems infatuated with that roadie."

"Yeah," Étienne chuckles. "I did notice."

"He's so grumpy, and she's so…*sunshiny*. It would never work between them."

"I guess we'll see. Stranger things have happened."

His fingers tighten around hers and he turns his head to face her. An invisible weight presses on her chest as the heat of his body presses against her. Every atom of her body begs for his lips.

"I'm so sorry," he says. "I know this is the second time I've thought you and Finn were… you know. I feel terrible about both."

Jordan inhales slowly, her pulse kicking up a notch, but if they're doing this, laying it all out, then she has to be honest. "Actually, the first time, you were right. At the wedding, when you said I couldn't stop looking at Finn, you were right, but it was just that one day." She presses her head back against the grey foam walls, staring up at the ceiling. "One moment he was good old Finn, the next he was the one who got away. And then as quickly as it started, it stopped. The day of your audition I was right back to normal. I can't explain it, I'm just sorry that I denied it to you."

Étienne shrugs. "You've got nothing to be sorry about. We're both adults. I was meant to be there on a date, you were tipsy and crushing on your best friend."

"*Temporarily* crushing," she reminds him.

"I can't blame you. Finn's a great guy, built like a Mack truck, and have you seen him in a suit? Woof."

"Stop."

"He bought me *donuts*, Jordan. You know I'm a slut for sweet things. If it doesn't work out between us, he's my backup plan."

She can't help but laugh as her heart lifts, soaring on hope and adoration. "Just know that it was an extremely temporary thing. It never happened before, and it hasn't happened since. There's only you."

His fingers curl a little tighter around hers. "I know. And I'm yours. Completely. We're going to mess up, we're going to get things wrong. But I need you, Jordan. I want to make this work."

"I want that too."

Étienne smiles as she raises his knuckle to her lips and kisses the back of his hand. "We should probably head down and let Finn know we're okay."

She nods, and he stands, offering his hand to help her up. But neither of them moves toward the door. They stand face-to face, and Jordan can't remember the last time she ever felt so wanted.

Hot breath blows softly against her hand as she raises it to his cheek, rasping his beard against her knuckles.

"I'm so sorry for ever doubting you," he says as he leans into her touch.

"I doubted you too. I fell for you so hard and so fast that it scared me."

He nods slowly closing his eyes as she caresses the soft cushion of his cheek. The slightest hint of pink still lingers, whether from the heat of the argument, or the same tingles of anticipation shooting through her body are coursing through his.

"One thing I don't doubt is that I love you." He opens his eyes and gently catches her hand, bringing it down to his lips. Softly, he presses a kiss to the tender underside of her wrist.

She can't bear the distance between them any longer. Pressing her body to his, she backs him against the wall, raking her fingers through his hair as she looks into his eyes.

"I love you too." She's breathless, need coursing through every sinew of her body, driving her as she takes both his hands in hers, lacing their fingers, and lifts his arms, pinning him to the wall.

His breath shudders out of him as he fixes her in a heavy-lidded gaze, full of hunger and aching desire. She leans forward, brushing her lips to his, and her body is aflame at their first touch. The world fades and it's only them, their lips, their hands pressed against the firm foam on the walls, the heavy rush of their breath. The only conscious thought she has is: *you.*

This is what she needs, *he* is what she needs, and as she kisses him hard, pleasure coiling through her body, she knows he's all she ever wants.

She lets go of his hands, but he obediently keeps them up, his lust-drunk eyes drinking her in as she stands back and pulls off his shirt, up and over his arms, revealing that soft, irresistible body she craves more than air.

She sinks her teeth into her lip as she caresses him, her hand gliding through the dark thatch of hair over his chest and stomach.

"Oh God," he growls, grinding his hips against hers, seeking release in the friction of his jeans. "Jordan."

His eyes flicker toward the door, the barest hint of nerves sobers him for just a moment.

"Are you okay with this?" She asks, circling his nipples with her fingertips in a way she knows is driving him wild.

"Very," he breathes squirming against her. "I'm just afraid they'll catch us."

"Then we'd better be fast." She sucks in a breath as his lip curls into a feral snarl. "Do you have a condom?"

"In my wallet."

He tilts his hips for her to take the worn black leather bifold out of his back pocket. There she finds a neatly folded strip of three condoms.

"Wait…" he tells her. She stops and takes a half step back, giving him space. He steps toward her, filling the distance between them. "I want you to come first."

She opens her mouth to protest that there isn't time, but she silences that voice in the back of her mind. Her pleasure is just as important as his. Her body trembles as the heat in his gaze consumes her, telling her that he agrees.

To hell with it.

"Get on your knees," she tells him.

Étienne makes a mental note to remind himself to buy Finn something better than a Muppets t-shirt. Kneeling in front of her, he's so lightheaded the room spins.

Jordan stands with her back against the wall, still dressed while he kneels shirtless. She lifts her skirt, and he can tell that she's wet and just as turned on as he is. His stiff cock aches as he breathes her in, as she pulls aside the cotton and pushes forward, pressing her perfect pussy to his lips. And the cry she gives as he kisses her is almost enough to tip him over into orgasm.

He clenches every muscle, trying to divert blood away from his cock as he licks her, as her fingers tangle in his hair and her hips bounce against the foam walls, setting the pace for him. She gasps and moans, before pulling down her underwear so he can taste her fully. Her skin is hot and slick beneath his tongue and it takes all of his self-control not to pull out his cock and start stroking himself.

She almost falls onto him as he takes a hand and presses two fingers against her entrance, sucking her clit as she cries out his name.

"Fuck, yes," she gasps, bearing down onto him, fucking his mouth and his fingers, the two of them focused on nothing but her. She braces her hands on his shoulders as she rides his face.

He matches her pace, pumping his hand into her, curling his fingers as she gasps and moans. And then she tenses, crying out as her nails dig into his shoulders, all but toppling onto him as she comes, as he licks every inch of her hot skin, drunk on the taste and the sensation of her.

"Sit back against the wall," she tells him as she rights herself. "Take your cock out."

He does as he's told, his hands trembling as he unzips his jeans and wriggles out of them until they're midway down his thighs. There's so much hunger and primal need in her eyes as she watches him, ripping into the foil square she took from his pocket and pulling out the condom. She steps over him, her wet, kiss-swollen pussy at eye level for a moment before she squats, straddling his hips and rolls the condom onto him.

When it's secured, she kisses him, sinking onto her knees until the heat of her brushes against the head of his cock.

The moment he enters her he swears his heart stops. The whole world stops. It's just them, their breath, the pleasure rolling through them as she bounces on him, rolling her hips and fucking him like it's the last thing they'll ever do. She takes his hands again, pins them to the wall, and explosions of excitement and pleasure detonate throughout his body. Delicious, perfect, everything he's ever dreamed about while he's fucked his own fist, while he's daydreamed of her. And somehow, it's so much more.

It's not just the sex, the physical pleasure of it. He loves her and she loves him, and he knows with all certainty she is it. And he is hers. Completely, willingly, he surrenders entirely.

As the pressure of his climax reaches its peak, she kisses him, biting his lip as he groans, pleasure consuming him. She holds him while he shudders, riding out every wave of ecstacy which rolls though his body, until he sits gasping and spent.

"I love you," he whispers, pressing his forehead to hers as he breathes her in.

She lets go of his hands and wraps her arms around him. "I love you too."

Gently, he lets down his arms, and wraps them around her, holding her to him. She's his, and nothing will ever come between them.

W hen she and Étienne eventually get downstairs, Finn is standing beside Beth at the front desk. The drummer narrows his eyes as they approach. "Well?"

"We still hate each other," Étienne shrugs. "We're going to go duke it out in the parking lot. You coming?"

A wide smile spreads over the drummer's face as he detects Étienne's sarcasm. "Sure, I'll pummel your face and Jordan can go for the groin, how's that?"

"Sounds like a plan," she grins, fighting back the urge to quip that she's already way ahead of him in that respect.

"I am sorry," Étienne says. "I shouldn't have believed him. I don't even like him."

"It's all good." Finn chuckles and shakes his head before turning his attention to Jordan. "Do you need a ride back home, or…?"

"No, I'm good." She lets go of Étienne's hand and heads toward Finn, stepping into his waiting embrace. "Thank you, for everything."

"Any time." The drummer holds her tight before releasing her and pulling Étienne into a spine-aligning hug. "If you ever need donuts again, you let me know, okay? See you both tomorrow. Be there by four or I'll find you, throw you both in the back of the van, and drag you onto the stage myself."

"We'll be there," Étienne assures him.

Jordan and Étienne leave the factory, hand in hand, the chilly night air whipping around them. A question burns at the back of her mind as they make their way toward his car. The thought of saying goodbye to him tonight fills her with dread. She wants to hold him, to spend the night wrapped in his arms, but perhaps it would be better for them to maintain some distance—

"Hey," Étienne says, turning a little to face her. "So, I'm wondering, if it's not too much too soon, would you maybe want to spend the night?"

The corners of her mouth tighten as she fights back a grin. Coming to a halt beside the car, she turns to face him fully. "I'd love nothing more. How about you spend the night at my place, and we cook breakfast together tomorrow?"

His face brightens, but his eyes are almost black in the moonlight. He raises an arm to slowly sweep his hand back through his hair. "That sounds perfect."

"Why is everything you do so irresistible?"

He shrugs, "Just part of the package."

"It's a good package," she says, closing the space between them so her chest brushes his. "Perfect."

He leans back against the door of his car as she kisses him, leading his hands to her waist. She could happily spend the night making out with him there, cloaked in the darkness of the factory parking lot. She has to remind herself it'll be so much nicer when they're back at her place.

"Come on," she grins, stepping back from him. "Let's go home."

Twenty-Two

The next day, they make it to the festival with plenty of time to spare. Jordan is jittery, filled with adrenaline in anticipation of the performance, ready to leave a full hour before they need to.

Arriving at the site for Ghoulfest is so much different this time around. He's elated, his heart pounding and feet all but skipping over the gravel. This is it. He's playing to the biggest crowd of his career, and hand in hand with the woman of his dreams. The sun has set, and the early bands are playing, their music blasting from the speakers, reverberating through his bones as they check in at the front desk and pick up their passes.

"Nervous?" Jordan asks, bringing his hand to her lips.

He shakes his head, but he is. His belly flutters as they approach the trailer, but he knows this time he'll sing his heart out. He'll sing to her.

His phone vibrates against his thigh for the eighth time that day, but he doesn't check. No doubt Dan has read his text telling him to shove his vineyard gig up his ass and is absolutely livid. Étienne fights back a chuckle. He'll find some other way to make money, even if it means giving up his dream for a little while. He'll work his way back up, somehow.

The sharp slap of the trailer door opening ahead draws his and Jordan's attention, and the big grumpy roadie hurries down the steps toward them. His eyes widen as he notices their approach.

"You're early," he mutters.

"Yeah, I like to be prepared," Jordan smiles. She glances toward the trailer. "Everything okay?"

The roadie's broad chest balloons as he draws a sharp breath. "Yeah. Just making sure everything is ready for you." He narrows his eyes at Étienne. "You're actually performing tonight, right?"

"Yeah," Étienne smiles, squeezing Jordan's hand. "I'm all set."

"Good." The roadie nods and hurries away toward the stage as Étienne and Jordan climb the steps and step inside the trailer.

"Happy Halloween!" Liz greets them enthusiastically, her eyes wide and wild, and her hair rumpled. "You're early."

"So are you," Jordan grins, setting her car keys and phone down on a countertop. "Everything good?"

"Great," Liz beams. "Fantastic, actually."

It's hard not to notice she's a little breathless. It takes all Étienne's composure not to let on he suspects what's going on. As the Vixen's arrive one-by-one he greets them and apologizes to each of them.

"You sure you're okay?" Mia asks, addressing both he and Jordan.

"We're great," he assures her. "Did Finn tell you what went on?"

"Yeah," the singer slings a shoulder bag off and lets it slump onto a chair. "Fucking Danny. If I ever see him, I'll…" She trails off letting her taloned hands speak for her as she mimics strangling him.

"Same," Liz adds.

"Get in line," Finn mutters.

Jordan shakes her head. "Don't bother, he isn't worth ruining your nails over." She takes out her phone to check the time. "Shit. We need to get ready."

The trailer becomes a hive of frantic activity as the Vixens begin rushing around, applying theatrical makeup and putting on their ghoulish costumes. Étienne stands back, watching and feeling a little underdressed in his simple black jeans and leather jacket. Even Finn, who has cut the sleeves off his "I heart Finn" shirt to show off his biceps, smudges liner beneath his eyes.

"Do you really think you'd get away with it that easy?" Jordan purrs beside him.

If he thought her outfit yesterday was a knockout, her choice today is damn near otherworldly. Yesterday she was elegant in lace but today she almost stops his heart in a black, figure-hugging leather corset and flowing skirts which are mid-thigh at the front but trail down to brush the floor behind her.

As long as he lives, he suspects he'll constantly be astonished by the sight of her. She's stunning, her hazel eyes accentuated by thick black eyeliner which flicks out at the corners. Her lips are blood red, and he can't think of anything more than having them on his body.

His throat grows tight as she leads him to a chair and

with a gentle push, commands him to sit. He'll happily spend the rest of his life obeying her, loving her, doing whatever she asks of him.

"Do you trust me?" she asks.

He nods. "Always."

She straddles his hips, the heat of her body and the intimacy of the gesture drying out his mouth. Those perfect red lips curve into a smile as she holds up a brand-new black eyeliner pen and leans in to kiss him. "I got you a present."

"Ah."

"Look up," she says softly, so he does as he's told.

The sensation of her applying the eyeliner makes his toes curl. Her breath is warm against his skin, her other hand resting on his chest as his heart thrums against it. He stays perfectly still, but from the sideways glance she gives him, he's almost certain she can feel his cock growing hard beneath her.

"Hey, Étienne," Finn calls over. "I'm on the forum right now and I think you're going to have a pretty decent fan club out there tonight. The fans are stoked."

A flutter of nerves rolls though him as he looks up at Jordan. She sits back, admiring her work as her teeth graze her lower lip.

"Ugh," she sighs, twisting the bottom of the eyeliner so the applicator disappears.

Étienne grimaces, "It doesn't look good?"

"It looks *too* good. The fans are going to devour you." She leans in and whispers against his ear. "And the second we're alone I'm tying you down and devouring you too."

His body bristles with need, his hands coming up to rest on her thick, irresistible thighs. Some part of him is sorely tempted to run away again, only this time he would take her with him.

"Lovebirds!" Mia calls, laughing as she adjusts the cups on her ornate metal bikini top. "This is a public trailer. If you need alone time, there are plenty of fields out there you can hide in."

A sharp knock at the door brings order to the boisterous trailer.

"*Five minutes*," the grumpy roadie calls from the other side. "*This is your five-minute call.*"

Jordan pulls in a breath and looks down at Étienne. Her pupils are blown wide and her cheeks flushed. "I guess we'll have to hold onto those thoughts," she says. "It's showtime."

T he distant roar of the crowd mirrors the thundering rush of blood in Jordan's ears as she climbs off Étienne's lap. He and Mia head to the back of the trailer and begin working on vocal warm ups as Jordan heads to the door. A sick, swirling feeling starts in her stomach, not just the usual pre-show flutters, but the absolute fear and certainty that something will go wrong.

"I'm just going out to check on my cello," she calls out toward the band. She still has a few minutes left before they're wanted on stage. "I'll meet you all up there, okay?"

Stepping out into the cool night air, she closes her eyes and drinks it in. The band on stage before them have finished their set, and pre-recorded music blasts over the festival's PA system, keeping the audience warmed up.

The head roadie might be grumpy, but he runs a tight ship, and so far, it seems every minute of the festival has gone according to plan. But there's something amiss. She knows by the crackle in the air, in the way her back bristles, the way her stomach squeezes.

"Well, aren't you a sight for sore eyes?" The voice sends a chill rushing through her body, answering that instinctive fear.

Straightening her spine, she turns to face him, and he's exactly as she remembered. Tall, lean body, broad shoulders, long black hair and beard. His dark eyes comb over her as though she's his to admire, the corner of his lips curling into a smile.

"Danny." She spits his name, wanting it out of her, wanting him gone. "What are you doing here?"

"Ex-bandmate troubles," he smirks. His eyes drop down to the top of her corset, and the tip of his tongue grazes his lips. "You know him, actually. Short, hobbit-looking mother-fucker. Kind of a diva. I need to speak with him. Your boyfriend just quit my band, and he's cost me thousands. I want my fucking money if I have to slap it out of him."

Her fists curl. "We don't have time for this."

"I decide what we have time for," he snarls, taking a step toward her. "I take it you got my message before I got kicked from the forum."

She despises that she flinches, despises that she involuntarily participates in his favorite game. But it isn't shame, it's anger, and she directs it all toward him. "Back the fuck off, Danny."

He laughs, "I always did know just how to play you, baby girl. Like a fucking maestro."

His derision means nothing, because she knows that beneath all that bluster, he's the one far from his home turf.

"I'm not scared of you." She steps toward him, her body tensing ready to fight. "And neither is Étienne."

"Keep telling yourself—"

"I'm not done," she says, holding up a finger to silence him. "You can slash my tires or find my house and paint vile words all over it. It doesn't matter. I can buy new tires, and your words just wash away. And while you're sitting alone sending messages to women you dated for a couple of months *eight fucking years ago* just know that the rest of us have moved on. We have lives, Danny. And you're not part of them."

Silence stretches between them. In the amber glow of the overhead lights, Danny's eyes are black, the vein in his forehead pulsing, as he stalks across what little space is left between them. He towers over her, a muscle in his cheek leaping as he sets his jaw. And despite it all, his posturing, the fact that she's dreaded this meeting for eight years, she couldn't be less afraid if she tried.

In the corner of her eye, she sees the hulking, black-clad figure of the roadie walking toward them. He cups his hands around his mouth and calls out. "Last call. Vixen's Wail to the stage."

The trailer door opens and the air fills with the sound of the band's excited chatter, which all at once falls completely silent.

Danny's eyes dart to the side, his scowl lifting into amusement. "Ah, the Addams family are here to back you up." He nods his head toward Finn as he backs away. "How's it going, Uncle Fester?"

"What do you want, Danny?" Finn growls.

"Jordan!" Étienne calls out to her as he jogs toward them, his eyes wide and panicked.

Jordan's knuckles are bloodless as Danny snickers. "There you are, you little fuck. You and I need to talk."

"I've got nothing to say to you, Dan," Étienne throws over his shoulder at the guitarist. He laces his fingers with Jordan's and gently tries to coax her away. "Come on. We don't have time for this shit."

He's right. Danny isn't worth a single second of their time. She turns to face her bandmates and gives them a reassuring smile.

"I'm not done," Danny growls, reaching out to grip Jordan's arm.

At his touch, her heart rate spikes, sending a flood of boiling blood coursing through her body. The world is pulled into sharp focus. There's only her, and him, his fingers gripping her upper arm. "Get the fuck out of here!"

Wrenching her hand free of Étienne's, she spins round to face Danny. Her fist darts out, slicing out and up through the air. Pain bolts through her hand and wrist as her fist connects with Danny's chin, throwing back his head and sending him stumbling.

"Ah, fuck," she hisses, shaking out her hand as Étienne stares wide-eyed. She's only vaguely aware of what's going on, the grating of gravel beneath sliding feet, Danny's cusses, the grumpy roadie's grunts as he drags him away.

"Holy shit," Étienne half-laughs in shock, taking her hand gently in his. "Are you okay?"

She grits her teeth. "Probably not the smartest thing for a cellist to do before getting on stage."

"No," Mia says as she approaches. "But I bet it felt fucking incredible."

"I'll tell you in a minute," Jordan says. "Once my body has stopped vibrating."

It takes a while for the adrenaline to ebb. The crowd roar, rhythmically clapping their hands together as they wait, filling the night with electricity.

Jordan flexes her fingers and fights back a smile. All those years she spent worrying about what would happen if Danny ever found her, and now she couldn't care less.

Étienne's thumb caresses her aching knuckle as he takes his place backstage where he can watch the rest of the band play their first four songs without him. "I'm so proud of you."

"I'm just me."

"You're strong and talented, beautiful. And you have a mean upper-cut."

She leans into him, closing her eyes as he kisses her, an oasis of comfort and warmth in the middle of a raging storm. "Well, I'm proud of you. I know it can't have been easy telling Danny you don't want to play with him anymore. Thank you."

He shrugs. "The money would have been nice, but the guy's an ass. I'll figure something out."

Out of the corner of her eye Finn and Mia exchange a look.

"Actually," Mia says. "We've discussed it, and the songs we have written for the next album would all work as duets."

Jordan's heart leaps. "You're serious?"

Étienne stares at the singer. "For real?"

"We'll discuss contracts after the show," Finn grins, clapping him on the shoulder as the roadie begins to usher them onto stage. "You're a Vixen now, Baby Bear. We've got your back."

"Holy shit," Étienne whispers. He turns to Jordan, beaming, his eyes searching her face. "I love you, so much."

She can't stop herself from stealing one last kiss before she goes, and as he melts against her, she's not sure she can ever let go of him. The crowd reach fever-pitch, chanting the band's name as she rakes her fingers through his hair, sending a shiver down his spine.

"I love you too," she tells him as she steps back, leaving him breathless, and looking at her like the world begins and ends with her.

***

She's incredible. Étienne watches her throughout their set, listening out for the somber tone of her cello, drawing comfort from it as goosebumps pebble his skin. Before he knows it, their songs are over, and it's time for him to join them.

"You ready?" a roadie with a bushy moustache asks, nudging his shoulder.

"Yeah." He nods. He has never been more ready.

"Alright. I've got guys positioned at all the exits ready to catch you if you run."

Étienne scowls. "Yeah, thanks."

The earth-shattering roar which greets him as he steps onto the stage is like nothing he's ever heard or felt. It pounds against his chest and brings tears to his eyes. And for the first time in a long time, he knows he's going to be okay. This is his life now, and he never would have believed it could be like this.

When he sings, he sings to her. Every note, every breath, every beat of his heart is for her, and the audience sings right along with him.

They call out his name, reaching out to him, and when he's done, they beg for more.

This is his life now.

"Thank you," he calls into the mic, his voice shaking as he fights back tears. There's only one thing on this earth more beautiful than the sea of people who lived every moment of the show.

The audience cheer even louder as Jordan stands and takes a bow, sets her cello aside and hurries across the stage into his arms. They damn near scream down the heavens as she kisses him, her body pressed to his, her fingers splayed across his jaw, holding him to her.

Not that she has to hold him.

He couldn't stop kissing her for anything in the world.

EPILOGUE

Jordan hurries down the hallway to their bedroom on tiptoe, balancing the laptop in one hand and clutching a coffee mug in the other. Étienne was still asleep when she left him for a Vixen's meeting that morning. She had tried to wake him, but he was exhausted from their tour-closing hometown show the previous night.

A year has passed since he joined the band officially, and he's not quite used to the pace of gig life yet, but it's almost noon and she can't wait any longer.

The warmth of the bedroom hits her like a tidal wave, and the scent of him makes her heart flutter. He's sleeping naked, belly down, and wrapped in the twisted bedsheets. His perfect round ass is just begging to be bitten.

Maybe later.

"Eti?"

He stirs and lifts his head. His eyes are bleary and narrow, his hair all rumpled from sleep. Ugh. She could just eat him up.

"What time is it?" he croaks.

"Eleven Forty-Eight."

He rolls onto his back, whispering, "Fuck. I missed the meeting?"

"Yeah, but it's ok I can fill you in." As important as her news is, she can't help but admire his body, the soft curves, the dusting of dark hair on his chest, stomach and thighs. It takes all her willpower not to pounce on him as she sets the laptop on the nightstand. "This is for you," she informs him as she hands him the mug.

He sits up, rubbing his eyes as he gives her a lopsided smile. "You're an angel."

"And you're a star," she grins, unable to hold back any longer. "Guess who's show got a glowing review from Armand Corvo?"

"You're serious?" His eyes widen.

Jordan bites back a squeal as she climbs onto the bed beside him and takes the laptop. "He's basically gushing over the Vixens. And look, he called your voice 'life-affirming', said that you're destined for greatness and he's watching you closely."

That praise is no small thing. Armand is brutal, often bordering on cruel, and as Étienne's eyes grow teary, she knows he feels the full impact of it.

"Shit," he mouths as he reads the full thing.

"Right?"

"Jordan?" He's on the verge of tears now, his cheeks reddening as he sets the coffee and laptop down. "Is this really happening?"

"It's real."

He glances up at the ceiling and pulls in a long breath. "Fuuuck."

She knows how much he wanted this. That reviewer

doesn't give out praise easily, and for all his swagger and confidence, Étienne doesn't fully see just how talented he is. "I'm so proud of you."

In response, he pulls the bedsheets over his head and disappears from view.

Jordan laughs and follows him, retreating beneath the blankets. Bathed in the soft white light filtering through the sheets he's somehow even more beautiful. His blue eyes scan her features as he smiles. Every moment she's with him is more than she ever thought possible. He looks at her as though he's witnessing a miracle, and she knows she looks at him the same way.

"You're famous," she grins.

His nose crinkles. "Nah."

She runs her hand over the curve of his chest and lets it rest above his heart. "Rock star."

He leans in to kiss her, his bare skin hot and all too tempting. She could happily spend all day here in bed with him, but she has a plan. One she doesn't want to put off any longer.

"Get dressed," she tells him. "I have something else I need to show you."

She hurries out of bed before he has a chance to see just how nervous she actually is.

Étienne's coffee is lukewarm by the time he gets into the passenger seat of her car, but he sips it anyway. "Where are we going?"

She reaches over and squeezes his thigh, biting her lip

suggestively. "It's a secret. You're in charge of the music though, so feel free to put on your non-stop A-ha loop."

He scowls at her playfully, even as he clicks 'play' on his 80s bops playlist. The dichotomy of his musical life isn't lost on him. It's synth pop and power ballads by day, blood sucking and coffins by night. But it works.

He didn't know life could be so perfect.

It takes less than an hour to reach their destination. The converted barn is perched high above the city on one of the foothills. It's a view he's familiar with, but he hasn't seen in over a year. The last time he was there it was covered in sparkling fairy lights, with lavishly decorated tables. "This is—"

"Finn and Beth's wedding venue," she says, unfastening her seatbelt and releasing a breath. "This is where we met."

He follows her lead and climbs out of the car. "Are we allowed to be here?"

"I called ahead," she smiles, taking his hand. "I wanted to come back here, to kind of do-over what happened that night."

A fluttering in his belly spreads to his chest as she heads around to the trunk of the car and takes out a thermos and a tall glass with a neon pink curly straw. "Hold this," she tells him.

He knows he has that goofy-ass crinkle nose smile as she pours out a bright blue liquid and urges him to take a sip.

"There's no alcohol in it, sorry. I wanted both of our heads to be completely clear this time," she says before pulling in a deep breath. "So, that night, I didn't want to tell you my name in case you found me. I just wanted to spend one night with you, no strings attached."

"I remember," he says, sucking the straw.

"Well, my name is Jordan Hayes, and I think it's fair to say there are a hell of a lot of strings binding us, Étienne Moore." She stops and reaches into her pocket. "Which is good, because I know how much you enjoy being tied down."

He almost drops the glass as she gets down on one knee, a blue ring box in her hands. Nestled inside is a simple grey band.

"It's made out of a meteor," she explains, her bottom lip quivering a little. "Because you're a star. And I want to spend every night with you if you'll have me."

"Yes, of course," he says. He drops to his knees, setting the drink on the ground. "Always. I'm yours."

"And I'm yours," she says, slipping the ring onto his fourth finger. "Forever."

He couldn't ask for anything more.

Sneak Preview

Keep reading for an exclusive preview of *Amped*, the next installment in the Vixens Rock series…

AMPED

The soundcheck blaring from the festival's speakers hums and pulses against Liz's sternum and her heart mirrors its beat. For four weeks Vixen's Wail have worked their asses off, preparing for Ghoulfest, the annual Halloween music festival. They're at the pinnacle of a decade-long grind to make it big. But it doesn't really feel like the start of anything.

For Liz Larkin, it could be an ending.

As she makes her way through the backstage area, she sidesteps out of the way of a bustling roadie, watching her feet to make sure she doesn't trip on the coils of cable.

Ghoulfest is the first big-ish festival the band have ever played at and yet, everything is somehow so…samey.

The same black loops of cable, the same flutter of nerves, the same scent of warm, sweating bodies. It might be a bigger stage, but it's just like any other show they've played. How was she to know when she joined at nineteen, that the band would become her entire life? An endless cycle of practice and performance, confidence in her ability as a keyboardist, which always grows into a jarring fear that she'll never be quite good enough. No matter how big the band get, it's always the same, just a little more polished.

Not to mention her appearance. Her long brown hair is always in the same flat ironed style, her clothes always black to match with the band's aesthetic. Black eyeliner, smokey eyes behind thick black-rimmed glasses. Nothing much has changed. When she was a shy teenager the baggy black clothes were a shield, but now…what she wouldn't give to dress in bright colors, dresses which hug her ample curves.

"Liz? Wait up."

She stops and turns in time to see Anya, the band's guitarist, hurrying toward her, darting through the backstage staff with effortless ease. Her shoulder-length auburn waves bounce as she jogs the final few steps. Anya is stunning as always, her bright blue eyes alight with excitement, the skin-tight lace of her top revealing just enough of her curvy figure that a gawping roadie trips over a box of wires. Coupled with her drive and determination to someday be counted as one of the greatest guitarists of all time, she's a firm fan favorite of the band.

"Can you believe it?" Anya grins, breathless. "Look at us, we're backstage at a fucking festival!"

"It's amazing," Liz replies as enthusiastically as she can while hoisting her ratty backpack further up her shoulder.

"Oh, shit what's wrong?"

Okay, so maybe all the enthusiasm she can muster isn't enough. "Nothing."

"Nerves?"

That works. "Yeah, just… you know."

"Gassy?"

Liz's mouth snaps shut as she scowls, much to Anya's entertainment. She isn't the only one scowling. The backstage staff are busy, hard at work and having to walk around her and Anya as they stand there chatting. From the frustrated tuts and mutterings, it's rapidly becoming apparent that they're outstaying their welcome.

"Come on, Finn said we have a trailer behind the stage somewhere," Liz mutters, turning back around to continue her journey.

"Exciting." Anya falls into step beside her. "So, what's up?"

I'm thinking about leaving the band. Those words press against the inside of Liz's lips, but she can't speak them, not yet, not on the biggest day of their careers so far. She's a good keyboardist, great, actually, but it was never meant to be her life. In a month she'll be thirty, a clear sign from the universe that she should find something which truly speaks to her.

Back home she has a stack of brochures for various colleges, neon pink post-it notes bookmarking the pages advertising their massage therapy classes. The brochures are all a couple of years out of date, but she's sure that for the most part all the information is still correct. It's a lot more work than she anticipated, not just learning the massage techniques, but about anatomy and first aid too. All in all, it would take hundreds of hours of training, but she could make a difference. She could help people.

"Nothing, I'm fine," she says in her usual bright tone. She glances out of the corner of her eye to see Anya raise a perfectly sculpted eyebrow at her. "I'm *fine.*"

"You're a horrible liar and you should be ashamed. It's okay to be nervous. This is a big fucking deal. There are going to be thousands of people out there—"

"And that's supposed to help my nerves?"

Anya shakes her head and rolls her eyes. "Well, I'm

excited enough for the two of us, and hopefully it's contagious."

"Like headlice?"

The air is knocked from Liz's lungs as she slams into something. Something big and solid.

She stumbles, reaching out for the closest thing she can grab onto to steady herself as she battles with gravity. But it isn't enough. Her legs crumple awkwardly. Pain shoots through her ankle as it twists beneath her, but she manages to stay upright, anchoring herself on whatever it was she crashed into.

Clutching fistfuls of warm black cotton—*oh no*—she raises her eyes to look at—*please no*—the man—*nooooo*—standing in front of her. He's over a head taller than her, husky and heavyset with big tattooed arms. His chin is covered in a thick brown and sandy colored beard, which almost completely hides his thick, sun reddened neck. His eyes aren't the striking blue of summer skies or azure waters. They're pale, somewhere between blue, green and grey, like weather worn cement. Maybe a mixture of all three. In any case, his eyes peer down at her, and they're definitely not happy.

That's fair. She wouldn't be either.

She lets go of his shirt, and presses her lips together. "Sorry. I didn't see you."

It's impossible that she didn't. This big, burly guy unapologetically takes up space in every direction. He's grizzled, magnetic, intimidating. And as her lips part and the world around them darkens a shade, she realizes he might just be hot.

She has always enjoyed a spot of mountain climbing.

The man doesn't speak. He just looks down at her as if

she isn't worth the expended oxygen, before carrying on his path. The words "Ghoulfest" and "Staff" are printed in pumpkin orange on the back of his shirt. He's a roadie.

"Doofus," Anya chuckles.

But Liz isn't looking at Anya. She can't tear her eyes from him.

Until now, everything has seemed so samey, but whoever he was, he's definitely something new.

Pain in the ass performers getting in his way. Jones smooths down his shirt over his soft, round belly and continues his search for his right-hand man.

"Anyone seen Imran?" he asks as he storms his way across the stage, ignoring the persistent twinge in his lower back.

Of course, no one answers him. They're all head-down, working their butts off to get this shitshow running as smooth as possible. The fact that he has a carefully cultivated reputation of being a hard ass doesn't help. People don't tend to talk to him and that's just how he likes it.

With a low growl he turns back around, glancing at his watch. Sweat pricks at his back, cold and clammy. He still has an hour before he can take more painkillers.

Distracting himself from the pain he notices she's still standing there, the woman who fell onto him. Her friend laughs as she buries her head in her hands and shakes her head. He'd be lying if he said she wasn't pretty. Full, curvy body, long brown hair, a little beauty spot above her lip. Even while this pissed off, he'd noticed.

Doesn't matter.

"Imran?" he calls, frustration growing.

"What?"

That voice is like a balm for his soul as he whirrs around to find his missing colleague. "Where've you been?"

"Trailer six. Can you believe they sent it to us without a single working lightbulb?" Imran shakes his head as his impeccably thick moustache twitches. "Unbelievable."

"It's sorted though?"

"Oh yeah. Phantasmagoria Euphoria are going to come out of that place with sun tans now."

Jones blinks slowly and shakes his head. "Phantasmagoria…?"

"Euphoria, yeah." Imran chuckles and runs his hands over his floppy salt and pepper hair.

Folding his arms over his chest, Jones taps the stage floor with the toe of his boot. "So where are we up to?"

"Two more bands for soundchecks. We still need to call catering and make sure they're still on for tomorrow. We have a busted speaker, three stage lights out, and I'm pretty sure Matt stole my pissing gaffer tape."

"Business as usual then?"

"Yup."

Pulling in a long breath, Jones makes a mental check list of everything he needs to do. For a part time job, this gig is a bigger pain in his ass than it has any right to be. Festivals don't come along very often, but even from his limited experience, he knows this one is a cluster. As soon as he arrived and saw that the artists had to walk through the same area his team were laying cables and carrying gear, he knew it was going to be a mess.

He glances toward where the woman stumbled into him. She's gone, but the sensation of her hands on him hasn't. It's been a long time since anyone touched him.

"Alright," Jones jerks his head toward Imran, rubbing the swell of his stomach as though he can erase the tingling. "If you want to take a break, I've got a handle on things."

"You sure?"

Jones nods, adding a gruff "Hurry the fuck up though," in case anyone suspects he's going soft. A sharp spasm of pain shoots through his back as Imran walks away.

Gigs were easy when he started out in his teens, but lately there have been a few too many back twinges and sleepless nights caused by cramping legs. The unwelcome but niggling fear that forty is only a couple of years away presses at the back of his mind.

As familiar and comforting as this job is, he can't keep doing it forever, and the money he makes at his other part time job at the bar isn't enough to support him. But what's out there for a guy like him? Big, grumpy, unsociable, covered in tattoos... there isn't exactly a plethora of suited CEOs lining up to offer him cushy office jobs. It's this or broke.

So, he plows through the pain as he works, climbing high onto the rig to fix the busted stage lights. It's cold up there, the wind whipping around him across the wide-open fields surrounding the festival site. Far below, set a short walk back from the stage are the trailers set aside for the bands. He doesn't allow himself time to wonder what it must be like for them; talented, pampered, living their dreams.

He closes his eyes and sucks in the cool air, gritting his teeth against the throb shooting from the base of his spine to the backs of his thighs.

"You okay, boss?" one of his team calls up to him.

The question makes him nauseous, because he isn't but he'd die before he admits it.

He's the big man, the tough guy. It's taken him nearly four decades to carve out that reputation, and he isn't about to give in now. His father and older brother went to great lengths to choke the softness out of him.

"I'm fine." He grits his teeth as he climbs back down, a cold sweat settling on his brow as he commands his shaking body to keep going. There's no way he's quitting now.

By the time the final band of the night, the headliners, Vixen's Wail are called onto stage, his vision is blurred around the edges and almost doesn't see her. The woman who ran into him is a member of the band.

His jaw aches from clenching it so hard, his palms marked with angry purple crescents carved by his fingernails, but his heart still manages to swell a little as she smiles up at him.

Behind her, her bandmates smirk and nudge each other and maybe it's the pain or the fact he's on hour twelve of a fifteen-hour shift, but it pisses him off. She's making fun of him. It happens a lot. Either people are terrified of him, want to fuck him, or mock him. The first two he's more than happy to cater to, but the third he can't stand.

He quickly dismisses any hope that she might be inter-ested in him and avoids eye contact all together. "Let us know if anything is missing. You've got nearly twice as many instruments as any other band we have playing so some-thing's bound to go wrong."

She flashes him another dazzling smile and says, "Thank you."

An ice chip deep in the arctic cavern of his heart begins to melt. Hers is just one of the thanks he gets from the band, but he clings to it. A tender thing he can keep to himself among all the pain and the cold, biting air.

When they head out onto stage, he allows himself to look. She's… well… gorgeous. He discovers she plays the keyboard, her fingers dancing as she makes her melodies, and he can't help but imagine what her light, skilled touch would feel like on his skin. His throat dries out as he watches her, and even though the music is blaring, pounding through the speakers, he hardly pays it any attention. His world encompasses nothing more than the sway of her hips as she plays, the way the dark brown curtain of her hair dances along with her as her fingers spider-walk across the keys. Every breath he manages to take is like pulling silk over jagged rocks.

Imran's voice snaps him from his trance. "Oh fuck."

Jones blinks rapidly, honing his attention on the rest of the stage, searching for the problem. One of the band's singers runs from the stage in a fit of stage fright, and the rest of the band are beside themselves. Just what he needs. Fucking divas.

Every second they delay feels like a year as the agony in his back twists and tightens. By the time the remaining members of the band stumble through their rehearsal and head back to their trailer Jones is barely even present.

"Can you close down?" he asks Imran, clapping his hand on the man's shoulder.

"Yeah, no problem." Imran squints at him. "Are you alright? You look like shit."

He doesn't answer. He can't answer. If he admits the truth, they'll fuss over him. They'll insist on taking him to the doctor.

The pain he can handle. What he can't handle is the thought of people thinking he can't take care of himself. He limps through the darkness behind the stage, hands shaking as he pops two tablets from their foil blisters. They're a low dosage painkiller, but he so rarely takes any kind of medicine that even that feels like an admission of failure.

Swallowing them dry, he heads over to a quiet spot behind the artist's trailers. No one will bother him there and he can't spend another moment standing. As gently as he can, he drops to the ground and lies on his back, squinting at the stars peering through the clouds in the blotted ink sky and waits for relief.

Acknowledgments

Thank you to Jake, my very own romance hero. I honestly couldn't do this without you, and I truly am thankful for everything you do to support me. I love you so much.

Thank you, Emily for your enthusiasm and wonderfulness. I never in a billion years could've imagined someone would cosplay my characters and you do it so beautifully.

Thank you to Jack Harbon for reformatting these books and making them so beautiful.

Thank you to all my lovelies over on Patreon, including the Vixens For Life, Emily H, Katie B, Melanie, Linda W, Janel A, Deanna S, and D Mayo-Wells. Your support means the world to me.

And thank you as always to you, if you are reading this. It has always been my dream to write stories, and having people who actually read them is just the most incredible feeling. If you have the time, I would appreciate a review.

ABOUT MARIE LIPSCOMB

Marie specializes in writing romances with plus sized heroines and plus sized heroes. She is the author of the *Hearts of Blackmere* and *Vixens Rock* series as Marie Lipscomb, and also writes short, bonkers, high-heat romances including *No Getting Ogre You* and *Santa Claus is Going to Town On Me* under the pen name M.L. Eliza.

Originally from Bolton, UK, Marie now lives in North Carolina, USA. When she's not writing, she can usually be found playing the same three video games on a loop (*cough* Dragon Age)

ALSO BY MARIE LIPSCOMB

The *Hearts of Blackmere* Series

The Lady's Champion

The Champion's Desire

Forever His Champion

The Harpy and The Dragon

The *Vixens Rock* Series

Rhythm

Amped

Writing as M.L. Eliza

No Getting Ogre You

Santa Claus is Going to Town On Me

www.ingramcontent.com/pod-product-compliance
Lightning Source LLC
Chambersburg PA
CBHW071246190726
48292CB00007B/2431